TUNDRA THREAT
SARAH VARLAND

D0186927

H HARLEQUIN® LOVE INSPIRED® SUSPENSE

LOVE INSPIRED BOOKS

ISBN-13: 978-0-373-44628-5

TUNDRA THREAT

www.Harlequin.com

Printed in U.S.A.

The wilderness was as treacherous as it was beautiful.

Will scanned their surroundings for possible threats, human or animal, as he followed McKenna.

She stopped by an unmistakable red stain on the brown earth where the bodies had once lain.

Knowing the blood had come from someone churned his stomach. But not as much as the thought that it could have been McKenna's.

The thought of little McKenna Clark all grown up and mixed up in a job like this played havoc with his mind. She was too young and inexperienced for an isolated post like this.

"Be careful." An uneasy feeling crept over him.

He heard the bang a split second before the bullet whizzed past.

"Get down!" he yelled to McKenna, taking her to the ground with him. He'd promised her he wouldn't let her get hurt and she'd almost been killed.

Last night's note had been a warning. Today, full understanding hit him with all the force of a charging male grizzly. Someone was trying to kill McKenna.

Books by Sarah Varland

Love Inspired Suspense

Treasure Point Secrets
Tundra Threat

SARAH VARLAND

lives in the woods in Georgia with her husband, John, their two boys and their dogs. Her passion for books comes from her mom; her love for suspense comes from her dad, who has spent a career in law enforcement. Her love for romance comes from the relationship she has with her husband and from watching too many chick flicks. When she's not writing, she's often found reading, baking, kayaking or hiking.

There is no fear in love, but perfect love casts out fear. For fear has to do with punishment, and whoever fears has not been perfected in love.
—*1 John* 4:18

Dedication

To my family—I love and appreciate all of you.

Acknowledgments

Thank you to my family. John, Mom, Dad, and Alison—you do everything from critique and brainstorm, to babysit, to answer odd questions about crime scenes. Josh and Timothy— thanks for providing a welcome break from writing now and then with your cuteness.

Thank you to Major Dennis Casanovus for answering research questions relating to this book and the Alaska State Troopers. Your help was invaluable and any mistakes or stretches are mine. Thanks also to Lindsay Moore for helping one of my characters stop the bleeding of a gunshot victim.

Thanks to my writing friends who have encouraged me with your friendship.

Thanks, Alice, for being a fabulous agent.

Thank you, Elizabeth, my editor, who has a special skill for making stories shine.

And thank you, Lord, again, for letting me live this dream.

ONE

A soft wind blew across the tundra, whispered through the grass and sent shivers up McKenna Clark's spine. The two bodies that lay in front of her were not the caribou or moose the wildlife trooper expected to find when she received a tip that someone might be poaching on the tundra south of Barrow. No, these bodies were definitely human. And they'd definitely been murdered.

Her stomach churned and swirled but she took a deep breath as she edged closer, closed her eyes most of the way and felt each person's wrist for a pulse, just in case.

Nothing.

She dropped the arm she'd last held, took several steps back and averted her eyes. She'd seen her share of senseless killing in her work, but this was the first time she'd seen a dead person outside of a funeral home. This wasn't what she'd expected when she'd signed up to be a wildlife trooper. She'd been through the trooper academy like every other Alaska state trooper, and knew her job was dangerous in a unique way. The wild animals she worked to protect were unpredictable and could pose a serious threat to her safety on their own. And anyone breaking hunting regulations had the potential to be dangerous to her. Those were all risks she understood and accepted will-

ingly when she took the job. But this? She'd never anticipated dealing with murder.

She forced herself to glance back down at the bodies, knowing she'd be asked more than a few questions
once she called this in. Especially about whether cause
of death was obvious. It was—in the form of a gunshot
wound on each.

"Everything okay?"

McKenna bristled at the voice of Chris, the pilot, who
was too close behind her for comfort. She whipped around,
wondering when he'd gotten out of the plane. "No. It's not."
He may be a contract-based employee of the troopers, but
his narrow eyes were full of something she couldn't identify, and the way he held himself made it seem as though
he had something to hide. She didn't trust him.

He held up his hands in mock surrender at her tone and
let out a low whistle when he caught sight of the scene in
front of them. "That's gonna need to be called in."

As though she didn't know that.

McKenna started toward the plane and the communi-
cations equipment, but paused when she realized the pilot
wasn't following her.

"Aren't you coming?" She pierced him with a gaze that
she hoped conveyed the fact that it wasn't really a question.

He took one more long look at the bodies, shook his
head and followed her. McKenna climbed into the plane,
relaxing slightly when the pilot climbed in next to her and
began preparing them for the flight. She wasn't sure what
it was about him that made her uneasy, but after a few
years on the job, she'd learned to trust her gut instincts.
She called headquarters and left a message to report what
she'd found, then leaned back against the seat, taking deep
breaths to calm her nerves. She wouldn't be able to fully

let her guard down until she was back in Barrow and away from this pilot and his too-watchful eyes.

The scene she'd just observed flashed before her and she wasn't able to suppress a shudder.

Though she had no logical reason to fear for her own safety, McKenna had a feeling that, back in Barrow or not, she wouldn't feel like letting her guard down any time soon.

"I got your message. You think you found a murder scene?" Captain Wilkins's voice was skeptical. McKenna squeezed her phone tighter. She could almost picture him frowning, bushy eyebrows pressed together, even though she'd only met him once—last week after she'd accepted the transfer and flown up here to the middle-of-nowhere.

"Yes, sir," McKenna said more calmly than she felt, knowing she'd stumbled over her words when she'd left her message and had likely confused an already abnormal situation even more. "I received a tip that someone had been poaching south of Barrow and had Chris fly me down to investigate. That's when I found the bodies."

McKenna exhaled, feeling a weight lift from her shoulders. This was almost over. She'd fill out a little paperwork, get that sent off before she left the office and be done with this case. Her heart ached for the dead men, for their families. For the lack of justice. But she'd done what she could. It wasn't her case. Other law enforcement agencies would look into it from here.

She wasn't sure she'd ever been so relieved. She sipped a long drink of coffee as she waited for the captain to tell her how she wanted her to handle her report. The coffee was cold and left over from that morning. But it was better than nothing.

"Thanks for letting me know. Keep looking into it and update me when you know more."

She almost choked on the coffee.

"Excuse me?" McKenna's voice pinched in her throat. "It's…it's not a wildlife issue, sir. I assumed I'd notify you and you'd pass it on to another trooper nearby. Or another agency."

"There are no regular troopers near there. Didn't they show you the map with currently filled trooper posts? You're it up there, Officer Clark. You were put in command of the Barrow post. That means someone had confidence in your abilities. Do the best you can and resolve this."

"But…"

"Work with the North Slope Bureau Police Department if you need to, but this is a state trooper investigation. And you have the lead."

McKenna knew she shouldn't argue, but when had that ever helped her keep quiet? "But I'm a *wildlife* trooper." She stated what should have been obvious, her mind flashing images from earlier in the afternoon that she'd prefer to forget. She couldn't handle deliberate crimes against people. That was her brother's expertise—he was an Anchorage police officer and loved every minute of his job. McKenna didn't know how he dealt with the hate. Hadn't she just told him yesterday when they'd talked on the phone about his latest case that she'd be terrible at that sort of work?

But the extra layer of steel in Captain Wilkins's voice made it clear he didn't care.

"You are. You've also been promoted to a position of authority. Poaching is often a motive for other crimes, like murder. It's not the first time we've had a wildlife trooper investigating a homicide. As I said, you have the lead, Officer Clark. I wish it hadn't happened your first week up here, but it did. Like it or not. Now, solve it or go back to the city."

McKenna heard a click. "Hello?" She pressed the phone harder to her ear. "Hello?" He'd hung up on her.

Solve it or go back to the city.

She hated herself for it, but for an instant she considered the second option. She loved the city of Anchorage. She'd hoped to make a difference doing a job she was passionate about while living her dream life in the city. That's what she *had* been doing until this "promotion" moved her out here into the bush. She was alone in this small town, with no colleagues to consult with, no superiors to go to for advice or mentorship. Nothing. It was just her. And Chris, the contracted pilot, if she counted him. Since the thought of him made the hair on the back of her neck stand up and she still couldn't erase the look in his eyes that had unsettled her at the crime scene, she wasn't inclined to think of him as someone on her side.

Should she go back to the city and admit that she wasn't ready for this opportunity, after all? No. She'd never been a quitter and she wouldn't start now.

McKenna hung up the phone and stared around at the tiny building designated as her "office." It was little more than a single-wide trailer, about fifteen feet long. But it had a coffeemaker, a desk and a space heater, and that really covered all the essentials. If she needed more she'd have to ask the police department for help or fly to another village or city where there was a regular trooper post.

She shook her head. This wasn't where she was supposed to be. Since early in high school, she'd started creating a list of goals for the year every January first. They weren't just resolutions, they were more specific than that. Like when she'd set a goal to graduate as valedictorian, which she'd eventually accomplished with a perfect GPA and quite a few advanced-placement classes. After she had her yearly goal list, she'd rework her five-year plan to include the current year and write out specific steps she'd need to take to keep herself on track.

This promotion taking her to the middle of nowhere was most definitely not on her five-year plan. Neither was pretending to be some kind of detective when she'd become a trooper, a *wildlife* trooper to help make sure wildlife in Alaska was managed and treated properly.

McKenna shoved the chair back and stood, frustration building in her. She hated when things didn't go according to plan.

Knowing there was nothing else she could do today, she shut off the light and let herself outside. Sunset wouldn't come for several more hours, since even September liked to remind the world that Alaska was the "Land of the Midnight Sun." McKenna kept herself alert as she walked to her car. She was new in town, with no idea who she should trust. And though the site of the murders had been miles away, Barrow was the closest town to the crime scene. Chances were good either the murderer or the victims had started out in Barrow. Questions terrorized her mind as she thought through the case again. Would the culprit kill again? Who might be the next victim? She had only a theoretical idea of how crimes like this worked. She'd been through regular training at the trooper academy but lacked the experience to back up what she'd learned. Maybe she'd call her brother later. He'd know what to do.

She dismissed the idea as soon as it came to mind. She loved Luke, but he already saw her as his baby sister. Calling him for help would just reinforce the perception that she needed him to take over and decide what was best for her. She'd been trying to break him of that habit since she was about ten years old, begging Luke and his best friend, Will, to take her with them on their adventures, and hear-

ing time and time again that she was too young. No, she'd
have to handle this herself. She was an adult.

McKenna climbed in her car, slamming the door shut
behind her and jamming her thumb against the lock button with more force than necessary. Hopefully she could
solve this case fast and wrap everything up before anyone
else ended up hurt.

Or worse.

Chills started at the back of her neck and chased each
other down her spine. She was as sure as she'd ever been
about anything—someone was watching her. Not just
watching. Observing. Studying.

Stalking.

She studied her surroundings. There were too many
places someone could be hiding. Under the trailer that
made up her office. Or farther away, in another car, behind a building.

It was impossible to know.

But she knew for sure she wasn't imagining it. Someone
had her in his sights. And since she'd never felt this way
before, it seemed safe to assume it had something to do
with the case today. Someone knew she'd found the bodies. Now they were following her.... Why? To see what
she did with that information?

McKenna didn't know. And she didn't know what to
do about it. Her mind tried to form a coherent prayer, but
part of her resisted. She wasn't in over her head yet. No
need to bother God about it now when she could still handle it herself.

She drove away, the uneasiness dissipating with the
distance she traveled, confirming further to her that
it hadn't been nerves, but that someone had been very
nearby, watching.

Maybe she was closer to over her head than she'd
thought.

* * *

Will Harrison shut his locker and blew out a deep breath.

"Rough day, Harrison?" His friend Matt Dixon entered the staff room and gave him a slap on the back as he walked by him.

"You could say that." The tourists he'd taken out today were hardly competent to hunt wildlife, as they'd paid to do through his employer, Truman Hunting Expeditions. He'd spent the day on edge, cringing every time someone picked up a gun. If it had been up to Will, he would have refunded their money and sent them home, but Rick, his boss, had made it clear that he'd accept whatever clients came their way, take them on a successful hunt and keep them safe.

Some days that seemed like a lot to ask for.

"Want to come over tonight? Lexi's cooking caribou stew."

Lexi's food was some of the best Will had ever tasted. But he shook his head anyway. "Thanks, man, but not tonight. Think I'm just gonna go home and crash." Maybe look at his bank statements again and see if he had enough yet to open his own guide service. One where sure, he'd have the stress of running his own business, but he wouldn't have the hassle of taking people he didn't feel comfortable giving guns to on dangerous hunting trips.

The door opened. "Good day, guys?" Rick Truman asked as he walked in. Matt nodded his answer, Will said nothing. There were some things he and Rick didn't see eye to eye on, and the clients were one of them. But overall he was a good boss, and besides, Will needed this job. Just until he finished saving money. Then he'd have his own agency, do business his way.

"I have a little bit of bad news. Those raises I promised

you guys?" He shook his head. "They won't kick in quite yet. It may be a few more months."

Will raised his eyebrows, waiting for more of an explanation.

"Seriously?" Matt shook his head. "Man. I was counting on that so Lexi could stay home when the baby comes."

Rick's expression was pinched. "Sorry. You've earned it. Both of you. But things are tight. Tighter than I thought they would be."

Will took in Rick's camos, which looked as if they'd never been worn, in contrast to his and Matt's, which had seen more than a few hunting and guiding trips. Maybe Rick had a different definition of "tight" than they did.

Rick sighed. "It's the economy right now. It's tough on everyone. But we'll push through it, take some more trips, come back out on top." He sounded as if he was reassuring himself as much as them, which made it easier for Will not to hold the lack of raise against him. "You'll see, guys."

"Don't worry about it." Will finally spoke up. "It's just money."

Matt nodded along with him, as did Rick, who cleared his throat and added, "Just money indeed."

"Listen, I've got to head out. I'll see you both tomorrow." Will waved on his way out the door.

Barrow Dry Goods was crowded when Will ran in to pick up dinner. Maybe he should have accepted Matt's invitation. Anything would have been better than eating alone at a two-person table in his kitchen, listening to the silence in the house that screamed of how alone he was.

Nights like this made him miss what he'd had—before the accident had taken Rachael from him.

He fought to push those thoughts away as he headed down the aisle toward the frozen foods. The past was long gone and he knew—he'd heard it often enough—that it was time to move on.

Still, as he surveyed his options and weighed them— frozen pizza versus frozen Chinese food—he couldn't seem to stop the memories from coming. Marrying right out of college had probably been half-crazy, but they'd been kids in love and unwilling to listen to anyone who thought they knew better. And they had several happy years. At least they were happy for Will. He'd always felt a little like he was holding Rachael back. She'd wanted to explore all of Alaska, take every adventure life had to offer, and he'd just wanted to live life with her. He wasn't afraid of taking chances, but he didn't seek them out the way Rachael did. The avalanche that had claimed her life on a wilderness skiing trip had been only two years after they married. Seven years ago in January.

He grabbed the frozen pizza and shut the freezer door, spinning around and running right into another customer. As his pizza and whatever she was holding crashed to the ground, Will berated himself for not paying better attention. He had to get out of his head. Stop living in years long past.

He brushed himself off, located his pizza and stood, offering a hand to the woman he'd run into. She took it and he helped her up.

And then the past was standing right in front of him again in the form of his childhood best friend's little sister. All grown up.

"Will?" McKenna's green eyes blinked their disbelief.

"What are you doing here?" The words came out harsher than he meant them to. He knew it as soon as her eyes narrowed and he saw in them a flicker of her Irish temper.

"Is this another one of those places that's too dangerous for a girl?" she retorted.

"You're seriously still mad that Luke and I wouldn't let you tag along when we were kids?"

"No," she said with a frown that clearly said yes.

"We were young. I didn't want you to get hurt." Not to mention the fact that Will had always thought she was kind of cute. Staying away from her as much as possible had always seemed like the best option—it broke about a hundred guy rules to have a crush on your friend's little sister.

"I could take care of myself just fine back then." She straightened even taller and lifted her chin, which stretched her height to an unintimidating five foot three. "And I can take care of myself even better now."

Will nodded slowly and lifted his hands in surrender. "Okay. It was just a question." He let out a breath slowly, willing his heart rate to return to a normal speed. He could still vaguely remember the day when, as a five-year-old, he'd gone over to see his best friend's new baby sister. He was the youngest in his family and hadn't been around babies much, so he'd expected her to be cute and quiet like babies on TV. Instead, her newborn face had been scrunched into a scowl and she'd screamed like she was being pinched.

She'd been a spitfire since day one, and nothing had changed.

"I'm here," McKenna began, "because I got a…" She stumbled over her words. "I got a promotion."

"And what is it you're doing now?" Will couldn't remember if Luke had said what McKenna was up to last time they'd talked. And though Will had wondered, he never felt comfortable asking.

Her gaze darted around them. "I'm a wildlife trooper," she said softly.

"Why are we whispering?"

She looked around again. Uneasiness crawled over Will as he felt his muscles tighten. "What's wrong?"

McKenna licked her lips, swallowed hard and then shrugged with forced casualness. "Don't worry about it."

"McKenna, just tell me."

It had been the wrong thing to say. She glared in his direction and tilted her chin in the air the way she'd always done when she was trying to look taller. "It was nice seeing you, Will. But I've got to turn in early tonight, so I'd better be going."

He wasn't done talking about whatever was making her act weird. Not even close. But the firm set of her lips made it clear she was finished with that discussion. At least for now.

"I'll be seeing you around, I guess," he offered. "Let me know if you want to get together sometime."

Her half smile was less than convincing. "I'll do that."

Without a backward glance she whirled around and strode off, dark red hair bouncing on her shoulders as she walked. He was alone. Again.

Will looked down at the pizza he held and shoved it back into the freezer. He wasn't so hungry after all.

TWO

McKenna's plan to get home early and get some sleep was a complete failure.

How was she supposed to sleep knowing she was once again living in the same town as Will Harrison? She'd had a crush on her brother's best friend since elementary school. There'd been a time when she had thought maybe he was interested in her, too—but she'd done nothing but embarrass herself that summer when she let a little of her interest be known. He'd only seen her then as a kid. Almost like his own little sister.

McKenna wished there was a way to douse cold water on the warm feelings seeing him caused to bloom in her heart. Maybe it would be easier if his eyes weren't the same electric blue of glacier ice and just as mysterious. Or maybe if his black hair didn't curl around his ears in such a perfect combination of messy and adorable.

Not that his looks mattered to her. She pulled the covers up tighter and rolled over, willing herself to fall asleep. Anything to get *him* out of her mind.

She tossed and turned for hours, looked at the clock more than once, hoping against hope it was morning. Beside her, her German shepherd, Mollie, raised her head, ears perking as she looked around. Apparently she couldn't sleep either.

McKenna listened but heard nothing. The entire day, so out of her comfort zone, had her on edge. She must be passing that uneasiness on to the dog.

The red lights on her digital clock blinked 1:02 a.m. McKenna tensed as she heard something that sounded like a door creaking. This time Mollie let out a low growl and McKenna motioned with her hand for the dog to stay put. It was probably nothing, after all. No sense in either one of them getting up.

More creaks followed, these sounding like someone walking on the old, probably rotting, floor. Most likely the intruder was a large man. McKenna knew someone her size wasn't heavy enough to cause the creaking. She eased herself out of bed, reaching into her nightstand drawer for her duty weapon, just in case. The dingy brown shag carpeting in the trailer that served as her house would muffle her footsteps. If there was someone there, she should be able to sneak out and confront him undetected.

Despite being told to stay, Mollie followed her to the edge of the room and at the next slight sound from the main living area let out a warning bark.

McKenna heard someone mutter something, then a clatter. She hurried down the hallway, but made it to the living room just as the door slammed and whoever had been in the house ran outside, concealed by the darkness that had finally fallen over the Alaskan sky. She watched out the window for a minute, hoping to see a car or something that would help her identify the person later, but she saw nothing. Defeat threatened to overwhelm her. Finally McKenna moved away from the window, making sure the dingy miniblinds were shut tight before she turned on the lights. The last thing she needed was uncovered windows with the lights on, making her shape an easy target.

After taking a few seconds to try to calm herself down,

she moved her weapon from a low-ready position pointing at the floor to directly in front of her, and prepared
to check the rest of the house. First she glanced into the
kitchen, which she could see from her tiny living room.
It was clear, she could see that from where she stood, so
she didn't bother to investigate closely yet. It only took
a few minutes to clear all the rooms, Mollie at her heels.
McKenna appreciated the canine company, but in truth,
Mollie was even less qualified for this than McKenna was.
At least McKenna'd had the training. Though the dog was
a German shepherd, a favorite of police departments everywhere, her dog had no training and was more at home
napping on the couch or trying to climb into McKenna's
lap than sniffing out criminals.

Heart still pounding, McKenna walked back to the living room, took a quick glance out of the corner of the
blinds. Still nothing there. She tried to relax some of the
tightness in her shoulders since the crisis seemed to be
over for now, but her body refused to cooperate. It looked
as if sleep wasn't happening tonight. Instead, she walked
to the kitchen to make a pot of coffee.

McKenna breathed a quick prayer that God would keep
her safe, deciding it wouldn't hurt to ask for a little help at
this point. She'd been in town less than a week. How she'd
managed to get caught up in a mess like this already was
beyond her. But she would handle it. She had to.

McKenna sat down at the kitchen table as she listened
to the comforting noise of brewing coffee, trying to take
deep, even breaths and work through what had happened.
She was assuming the intruder was the person responsible for the bodies she'd seen on the tundra, but why had
he come to her home? Surely he wouldn't kill her just for
seeing his crime scene. Would he?

She stood up to retrieve her coffee then moved back to

the table, setting her mug down as she reached to replace the chair that the intruder had knocked over in his hurry to escape. She bent to lift it and noticed a small index card on the floor next to it, blank side up. Hesitantly, she reached to pick it up, just by the corner in case there were prints, and flipped it over on the table.

When she read the words, she dropped into her chair immediately, reaching out to pet Mollie to try to calm her racing-again pulse.

A shiver ran down her bare arms and she read the words again, this time aloud. "'Go back to where you came from and forget what you saw today, or the next body found on the tundra will be yours.'"

Glancing at the phone next to her, she let out a sigh. She had to text Luke for help. She was now officially in over her head.

Somehow sleep must've finally found McKenna, because when she woke up from her cramped position on her living room couch, the clock said it was past six.

Still alarmed from the previous night's events, she glanced around the room to see what could have woken her. Was she just done sleeping, or was it something else?

Something or someone banged against her door with increasing force. McKenna jumped. Mollie lifted her head in alarm, then looked to McKenna to gauge her reaction. McKenna took a deep breath. Her assailant, back to shut her up forever? Reason stepped in. No, if he'd wanted to kill her, he'd have done so already. He must have meant to warn her.

For now.

Besides, criminals didn't knock. Usually. Still, she crept toward the door, stealing a glance out of one of the front windows to see…Will?

She opened the door to him, noting that he looked half-asleep himself. "What are you doing here?"

"Good morning to you, too. That seems like a common question for us, doesn't it? How about you let me in and pour me some coffee and I'll answer you."

She hesitated, looking down at her yoga pants and old T-shirt from a 5K she'd run several years back. Even if there could be nothing between them, her pride would rather he not see her like this.

Will nudged the door. "Come on, McKenna. I've seen you look worse. Just let me in." He pushed the door open farther and stepped in, shutting it behind him and turning the lock.

He looked around the room and shook his head. "Nice place you've got here."

"I recognize sarcasm when I hear it. Even if I am barely awake." She tossed the words at him as she walked to the kitchen. She'd rather not comply with his request—no, demand—to make coffee, but she could use more herself and she wasn't about to do without just to spite him.

"Seriously. Did you look for the house that looked most likely to have been the site of a murder?"

"Yeah. That was totally what I was going for." So maybe the trailer was on the shabby side, but it meant she could save her money. That way, when she finally ended up in Anchorage, she could afford someplace nice. She glared in his direction. "Again, why are you here? Did you have a purpose, or are you just supposed to be a little ray of sunshine on this cloudy morning?"

The smile fell from his face. "Your brother texted me." His tone was heavy. Serious.

"Oh." McKenna looked away, went back to fixing the coffee. Great. She'd texted Luke to ask for advice because she was independent not stupid. Luke had said he'd get back to her with some suggestions for keeping herself safe and solving this and that was what she needed. Not Will Harrison showing up and seeing her all damsel-in-distress.

That was the last way she wanted him to see her. Maybe second to last. Right up there behind "like a sister."

"I don't know what he told you," she began as she set a mug in front of him filled with the hot, black liquid. "I just needed to talk to him about a few things last night. I'm fine right now. There was no need for you to rush over here before sunrise looking like you haven't slept in a week." She surveyed his sleepy eyes, the stubble on his well-defined jawline. "*Did* you sleep?"

"I slept fine. Until I got his text."

"Which was when?"

"Two."

"So you haven't slept since two?"

"Couldn't." He shook his head. "I came over here as soon as it seemed late enough to not be rude." Some of the seriousness left his face as his mouth stretched into his trademark charming smile, the one that had made all the girls in high school swoon. "No need to welcome you to town by taking away your beauty sleep."

"Yeah, because clearly I need every bit, right?" she muttered as she poured her own coffee.

"I didn't say that. Besides, I figured if I came over here at a decent hour I could talk you into fixing me some coffee. And maybe breakfast? I think there's a jar of pickles in my fridge. And maybe some sour cream from a few months ago. But nothing that seems edible."

"Fine. I'll make pancakes. You'll tell me what my meddling brother told you. Then you can go back home and go to sleep or do…" She realized she had no idea what he did for work these days. She'd lost track—intentionally. Keeping up with him had hurt too much. She pulled her attention back to the present. "Or do whatever it is you do. I have to get to work. I have a lot to do today. Things are crazy."

Will leaned back in his chair. "Sounds good. And it's that part about work being crazy that I wanted to talk to you about."

Will watched McKenna's eyes narrow, knew he was dancing dangerously close to the line where she was concerned, between her teasing him back and giving in to her temper. She was annoyed he was here, that much was clear, but he couldn't tell if it was because she really didn't believe she needed help, or because *he* was the one offering.

He'd always thought they had a pretty good relationship. No one had ever understood him the way McKenna had always seemed to. In fact, if she'd been anyone else, he'd have claimed the first dance at the Seward High School Homecoming her freshman year of high school when he was a senior and seen where their attraction and connection could take them.

But she was his best friend's little sister. So he'd done what he should and stayed away, keeping their friendship to teasing and the occasional long conversation down by Resurrection Bay, when he'd escaped the house to get away from his drinking father and she'd be down by the water, just watching the waves.

Then he'd gone to one year of college in Anchorage, fallen in love with Rachael, and that was the end of that.

Or so he'd thought.

"Whatever Luke told you is probably not true."

"Because your brother is so known for not telling the truth."

McKenna laughed and Will joined her. Luke was one of the most brutally honest people he knew.

"Obviously that's not it. But anything I told him certainly didn't include 'hey, and could you send Will over here before the sun is up to demand pancakes and talk to me about my job?'" She stirred the batter and looked back up at him. "So I can only assume he exaggerated something. Either that or you really are starving."

"He told me you texted him last night asking for advice because someone broke into your house, possibly connected to a double murder you stumbled upon on the tundra yesterday."

Her face fell. Apparently she'd wondered if Luke had told him all of that and he had confirmed it. But why did it matter to her if he knew? Didn't she know he'd want to be there for her as soon as he heard she was in trouble? Was she that determined for them to stay out of each other's lives?

"So here I am, wanting more details and to see how I can help."

"That's the thing, Will. I'm a big girl now. I don't need your help." She sighed and softened her tone. "It's nice of you to care."

"Of course I care. You and Luke have always been like family to me."

Out of the corner of his eye, he thought he saw her flinch.

"At least tell me about it. Luke didn't give details."

She kept pouring pancakes onto the griddle, not acknowledging him for a minute, then finally nodded, then exhaled. "Okay. I got here less than a week ago. Yesterday was my first day working and I received an anonymous tip about illegal hunting going on south of here. I had Chris— he's the pilot who's supposed to fly me around when I need it—take me to where the caller had described. We hiked quite a bit, searching for signs that people had been there. We eventually found some, followed the trail, and…"

Will watched her swallow hard, saw the way her face paled to an unnatural shade of green. She was tough, but crimes like these weren't supposed to be part of her job description.

"And then last night someone broke into your house? Do you think the two incidents are connected?"

She set a plate full of pancakes down on the table in front of him and laughed, a laugh that was entirely without humor. "I'm sure they're connected."

"How?"

She slid a piece of paper across the table to him, and as he read the overtly threatening words, his stomach clenched.

No question, McKenna needed his help. And she was going to get it. Like it or not.

"You're thinking something." McKenna pointed out the painfully obvious after several minutes of watching Will's thoughts work out in the expressions on his face.

"I am," he admitted between bites of pancake.

"So… Out with it."

"You're going to hate it."

"You don't know what I'll hate and won't." McKenna folded her arms across her chest.

"No, I'm pretty sure you're going to hate this."

"Are you going to let me figure that out for myself or not?"

He paused. "Let me fly you around."

"Fly…me…around… Wait, wait, on a plane?"

Will laughed and it lit up his face. She tried to ignore that and focus on the fact that he was plotting to take the little independence she'd gained by stepping into her life and taking over. He could call it "caring" or whatever else he wanted to, but she knew what he was doing. Exactly the same thing Luke would be doing if he was there. Would the two of them never let her be in charge of her own life?

"Yeah, on a plane. I'm a pilot. Luke didn't tell you?"

"We don't really talk about you." McKenna shrugged, unwilling to admit the various reasons she didn't ask her brother for updates on him. As a brother, Luke was as good as they came, but she'd rather crawl under a rock and never come out than have him find out about the crush she'd had on his best friend.

"I'll try not to be too hurt." There he went with the teasing again. "Piloting is what I do up here. I work for a guide service, shuttling people around on big-game hunts."

She raised her eyebrows. "So I'm here to save the wildlife and you're up here to shoot it?"

He bristled. "You know me better than that. I care about protecting the wildlife, too. But as long as the laws are followed, I don't think there's anything wrong with hunting, especially for someone who's planning to eat what he gets."

And Will did that, too. McKenna respected that about him.

"Fine," she conceded. "And about your offer, thanks, but no. I have a pilot assigned to shuttle me around. I don't need the help." Although she did feel a sinking in the pit of her stomach, something like a large block of glacier ice, when she thought about being alone with Chris again. Something about the way he studied her every move… She shivered.

"I'm not talking about just being your pilot. Officially, sure. But I can be an extra set of eyes for you. You can fill me in about the other details of the case as you learn about them and I can help you solve this thing so you can move on with your life and get out of this town."

She jerked her gaze up to meet his. "Get out of this town?" Had Luke told him how much she'd dreaded this "promotion" and all it meant? She was going to have to rethink her choice of confidant pretty soon.

"You always planned to get out of Seward and to the city as quick as you could. I'm guessing that hasn't changed?"

Was it her imagination, or was that hope in his voice? McKenna shrugged. "I do prefer Anchorage to small towns." Prefer was an understatement. Kind of like saying a polar bear was large.

"What do you think?"

"About you flying me around? I already told you no."

He raked a hand through his curls and shook his head. "You're too stubborn for your own good, do you know that? You have to learn when something is too much for you and let people help."

"What if I don't think it's too much for me?"

"People are dead, McKenna. And there's a good chance the guy who killed them, shot them in cold blood, was in your house last night. You're on your own out here. You have no backup. Let me help."

Several beats of silence passed as the truth of his words sunk in. She felt her shoulders sag slightly. "You can't just go around demanding things of people. I have a right to make my choices."

"So you want me to offer you something and then say please?"

She sighed. "No, but you know what I mean."

And then Will's hand was covering hers, setting her pulse racing twice as fast as it had during the scare the night before and making her hand tingle as though a thousand tiny fireworks had exploded inside. She gulped and tried to remind herself that they were just friends. And that they'd never be anything more.

"So. How about it. Let me help?"

He had the decency to phrase the last bit as a question, though she suspected he was just humoring her. Still, a look at his eyes showed that as he'd said, he did care.

"And how much are you charging?"

He looked insulted that she would ask. "I won't charge you anything to fly you around. I'd like to be reimbursed for gas, if the troopers have the budget for that, which I'm assuming they do. But for the flying time? There's no need."

"Don't you need your boss's permission to use the plane?"

Will smiled. "It's mine."

"Okay, but this can't be full-time for you—you need to work."

"Yes," he agreed quickly, and she thought she might have found her way out of this situation until he spoke up again. "But the next few weeks are pretty easy for me. I can fly for you around the schedule I already have set up at work. There's plenty of time."

McKenna was running out of logical arguments.

His offer made sense. But she wanted to refuse him. Had to.

Then she thought about the man who'd broken into her house, the quick glimpse she'd caught of the back of him. He was tall; she knew that. So was the pilot she'd been using to fly her around the North Slope Bureau. If she turned Will down, she'd have no choice but to continue using Chris for transportation and that was just about the last thing she wanted to do.

While Chris had been working on a contract basis with the troopers, he was paid by assignment. McKenna didn't think there would be a problem calling Captain Wilkins and requesting permission to give the contract job to Will instead. He'd have to pass a basic background check of course, but since he wouldn't be doing any on-the-books investigating, just serving as a chauffeur, that was all that would be necessary.

She felt chilled through when she thought about boarding a plane with Chris again. Hadn't she felt uneasy around him yesterday, felt as if he was watching her reactions more than he needed to? One thing she was sure of—law enforcement officers of any kind were supposed to trust their gut instincts. And hers said that there was more to that pilot than met the eye.

That could spell disaster for her.

On the other hand, the extra time with Will might be difficult. The last thing she wanted was to fall into some childish attraction to him again and embarrass herself. Surely she was past all that, though. As adults, their personalities were far from compatible. Will's being comfortable with changing plans last minute and flying her around proved that. He'd always been easygoing, ready to take life as it came. And McKenna liked to have a plan. A relationship between them wouldn't work, so surely she could remember that and keep from humiliating herself in front of him. And if nothing else, accepting his offer would give her a chance to prove to him once and for all that she was a strong woman, capable of taking care of herself. If he got the message, he might even convince her brother to knock off the overprotectiveness. Okay, that wasn't very likely—but she could still hope. There was a lot she didn't like about this promotion, but maybe it would give her that longed-for chance to show the people in her life what she was capable of. It was worth a shot.

McKenna took a deep breath. Nodded. "Okay. Let's do it."

And as another brilliant grin split Will's face, her stomach simultaneously danced and churned as she wondered what she'd gotten herself into.

THREE

McKenna eyed the plane in front of her and then looked back at Will. "You seriously know how to fly this thing?"

He just laughed and continued his preflight checklist. "Would I have offered to help if I didn't?"

She shrugged.

Will brushed off his hands and stood from where he'd been bent looking under the plane. "All set, I think."

"You *think*?"

He laughed again. "We're all set. I'm sure of it. I always check everything before I go." His face sobered. "Better to be safe than sorry and all that. I'm extra careful because a buddy I took lessons with crashed his plane a year or so ago and didn't make it. Neither did his passenger."

"I'm sorry to hear that…. Especially right before I climb into that thing with you."

"I'm always careful, that's what I'm telling you. Besides, I'd never let anything hurt you, McKenna."

Years ago, in the throes of her ridiculous crush, she'd have seen those words as some sweeping romantic promise. Now she knew better—it was just more evidence that he saw her as someone to be protected. She bit back the urge to remind him that she was the one with training and an actual mandate to serve and protect and she didn't need him to treat her like a fragile, sheltered princess. But there was no need to start the day with an argument, no matter how frustrated his attitude made her.

They climbed into the plane and Will taxied down the runway, easing the nose of the small aircraft into the air seamlessly. McKenna let out a breath she hadn't realized she'd been holding.

"All right. So we're headed south."

"Yeah, southeast." She gave him the coordinates for where they'd found the bodies.

"And all that's your territory? That's a pretty far range for one person to cover."

McKenna nodded. "Yeah. I guess that's why this was technically a promotion, because it's more responsibility."

"Where's the closest trooper besides you?"

"Kotzebue." She named a town on the western coast of Alaska, hundreds of miles away and not connected to Barrow by anything resembling a road.

"Not exactly close."

She shook her head. "Not at all."

"What if this situation escalates?"

McKenna shrugged. "I work harder, I guess."

"So you're on your own then."

"I can handle it."

"I never meant to say you couldn't."

Conversation lulled then. Not a comfortable pause, but an awkward silence where McKenna could feel Will weighing his words and deciding what was safe to say. So maybe she'd overreacted, but it had seemed as if he was implying she couldn't handle things on her own.

The bodies she'd seen the day before flashed before her eyes, and terror rose for a brief moment in her throat, but she shoved it down. She could handle this. She could.

"What are we looking for when we get there?" Will

had apparently decided to go with a change of subject, which McKenna thought was smart of him. He'd apparently learned something about women in the years he'd been married.

"I...I don't know," she admitted. "I talked to Captain Wilkins yesterday and he told me he'd sent in paramedics to handle the scene. There's no medical examiner in Barrow, so paramedics take care of it."

"You didn't have to stay until they got there or anything? Make sure the crime scene wasn't tampered with or corrupted?"

Wilkins had asked the same thing of her yesterday—why she didn't stay. She'd stuttered out an explanation for him, telling him how shocked she'd been and how she hadn't known what to do, but it had only sort of satisfied him.

"You were supposed to," Will said with understanding after reading her silence. How could he do that? Was she that transparent, or could he still read her thoughts well after all those years? They'd been close the summer after his senior year, had spent long hours talking by the water as the midnight sun shone down on them. Then he'd left, taking McKenna's heart with him. No, scratch that. She'd tried to offer him her heart, attempted to awkwardly confess her crush to him, but either he hadn't understood what she'd been trying to say or he hadn't felt the same. When he left, he left her, her bruised ego *and* her heart behind.

"Yeah." She exhaled. "I was supposed to."

"It's not normal for your job, though, having to deal with all this."

She didn't like the fact that he was now privy to one of her failures. "It doesn't matter. I should have known. I've had the training."

He said nothing in reply, just kept piloting them across

the vast wilderness. It was beautiful out there, down below their tiny airplane. Braided rivers rushed across the green and gold of the tall tundra grass, and the fireweed, which had bloomed almost all the way up, indicating that summer was over and winter would arrive soon, provided a stunning dark pink contrast. Taking her cue from Will, McKenna sat in silence, enjoying the view and sorting through case details in her head.

"Is this it?"

McKenna confirmed the coordinates with him and noticed details of the landscape that looked familiar from yesterday.

Will landed the plane smoothly, allaying her fears about his flying abilities, at least for today. After he'd finished his post-flight duties, McKenna led the way. "It's about... probably half a mile this way," she told him as they started to walk.

"Why didn't we land there?"

She stopped in her tracks. "You know what? I don't know why I didn't think of that."

"This really isn't what you're used to, is it, city girl?"

Maybe it was the "city girl" comment. Or maybe it was the compassion in his tone. McKenna wasn't sure. All she knew was that she'd messed up again, in front of one of the people she'd most like to prove her competency to. "I can handle it fine, Will," she ground out between clenched teeth. "I messed up a couple of times. But I won't again." She prayed it would be true and silently begged Will not to contact any of the people he must know to tell them she wasn't up to this job. People's recommendations went a long way up here in the middle of nowhere.

Her job was on the line if she didn't get it together. And even if the location was less than ideal, this job was the only one she'd ever really wanted.

"I can handle it fine," she repeated again with more firmness, not sure who she was convincing.

Will threw up his hands in surrender. "What is with you? It was just a comment—I didn't mean anything by it. Do you want me to take you back to Barrow and forget my offer ever existed?"

Yeah. That was exactly what she wanted. Except when the wind crept across the tundra, whispering through the grass and taunting her with the fact that it knew and had seen what had happened here yesterday, chills invaded her entire body. She couldn't come back here with Chris.

She might not relish giving Will a front-row seat to her fumbling attempts to handle the case, but she trusted him. With her life, if necessary.

And for now that would have to be enough.

What was it she thought she had to prove? Will wondered as he walked behind her, scanning their surroundings for possible threats, human or animal. He'd spent enough time in this wilderness to know it was as treacherous as it was beautiful. But even as he tried to remain alert to his surroundings, his eyes kept returning to the woman beside him.

McKenna hiked along without another word to him, which left him time alone with his thoughts. More time with them than he wanted, if he were honest.

Thankfully, she stopped soon, pointing to an unmistakable red stain on the brown earth that he couldn't have missed even if he'd tried.

"The paramedics took the bodies to Anchorage this morning."

Will didn't consider himself to have a weak stomach—look at what he did for a living. But something about knowing the blood had come from *someone* instead of something, like the animal blood he was accustomed to seeing, churned his stomach.

But not as much as the thought that it could have been McKenna's. What were the chances that whoever had committed the crimes had still been around yesterday, watching the investigation of his crime scene? Was it just arson where people did that, or was it all crimes?

The thought of little McKenna Clark mixed up in a case like this that could end up getting her killed played havoc with his mind. What had her superiors been thinking, putting someone as young and inexperienced as she was in an isolated post like this, where she'd be facing any danger alone?

"Be careful," he said as he looked around again, not liking the uneasy feeling that had crept over him.

"I am."

He moved closer to her.

"Really, Will. I'm fine."

He watched as she bent low toward the ground to snap pictures of the scene with a digital SLR camera.

"Is everything like it was when you left? Minus the bodies?"

She considered his question and nodded slowly. "As far as I can tell." She moved the camera around, surveying the area through the viewfinder as though looking through the apparatus helped her focus her mind on the scene. She snapped pictures of the surrounding area. Finally her gaze rested on a patch of grass about ten feet from the crime scene itself.

"Something else was dead."

"What?"

She moved closer to whatever she'd noticed and Will followed. The grass there was stained red, too, though the stain wasn't as large. In fact, this puddle of dried blood much more resembled what he saw on hunting trips.

"Another body?" Will asked. "Or do you think…"

"They were hunting," McKenna said aloud, finishing the thought. "But someone moved whatever they killed."

He nodded. "I think you're right. Caribou, maybe? That's what's usually hunted in this part of the tundra. And the flat spot in the grass looks like the right size."

She nodded. "I think so." She leaned forward, snapped a picture, and then snapped pictures of the entire surrounding area.

Will heard the bang a split second before the first bullet whizzed past his head.

Rifle fire. Aimed right at them.

"Get down!" he yelled to McKenna, reaching his arm out to take her down to the ground with him. To his surprise, she didn't protest but lay still where he'd tackled her onto the ground. Several more bullets flew overhead and Will fought panic when he realized how close the shooter had been to hitting them. He'd promised McKenna he wouldn't let her get hurt, and she'd almost been killed.

Whoever was doing this meant business.

Will felt McKenna fumble for the weapon at her holster as he went for his own, usually used to protect him and his clients from animal predators. "Can you tell where the shots are coming from?" she asked.

"No. You?"

"Behind us somewhere. That's all I can tell."

It was a wonder she could tell that. The wide-open tundra was a sniper's paradise. The killer had probably waited out here, expecting McKenna to come back and investigate, and completely concealed himself in the tall grass while his target was open.

In fact, once he thought about it, it wasn't surprising at

all that someone had fired on them. It was surprising that he or she had missed.

"I don't want to fire until I know his position." McKenna's words were tense. "I don't think there are any more people out here, and the gunfire would have scared off the animals, but…"

"But you never fire until you're sure what you're aiming for," he finished for her, knowing the firearms safety rule well from trying to drill it into irresponsible clients with more money than sense.

They lay side by side, each with weapon out and ready, but the shots had stopped.

"What now?" Will asked in a whisper after a minute, when it became clear that the shooter had given up for the moment.

"We're half a mile from the plane."

"Assuming he didn't find the plane and do anything to it."

The panic in her eyes made him wish he hadn't voiced the dark thought. "I'm sure it's fine," he said with more assurance than he felt. "I think we just wait here for a while, until we're sure he's gone."

"Then just stand up and hope we don't get shot?"

"Yeah, that's all I've got. You?"

"Nothing better."

By what felt like a mutual unspoken agreement, they lay there without speaking, each of them keeping their eyes fixed on places a threat could approach from. Will wasn't sure how much time had passed before McKenna finally whispered that they should try to make it to the plane.

"I think you're right," he agreed, knowing that the longer they stayed out, the greater the danger they'd face from animals out here as well as whoever was trying to kill McKenna.

Full understanding hit him with all the force of a charging male grizzly. Someone was trying to kill McKenna. Last night's note had been a warning. Now the danger was real.

"Ready?"

He pushed the troubling thoughts from his mind, knowing distraction could get you killed out here. "As I'll ever be, I guess."

They stood slowly. Will still couldn't shake the feeling they were being watched. And this time, when the next bullet cracked through the air, before he could take McKenna down, she yelled, "Run!" and took off in the direction of the plane.

Will ran after her, both of them sprinting fast enough to have made their high school track coach proud. The uneven ground of the tundra seemed to be working against them—spraining an ankle or worse would be too easy out here.

The shots continued, but McKenna showed no sign of slowing. "Get down!" he yelled, believing it was their best chance of surviving but knowing he'd never take cover if she wasn't going to.

"We can't!"

Stubborn woman. Panic clawed at him again, as it had when they'd walked up on the scene and he'd realized how much danger it could put McKenna in. She was too inexperienced for this.

He'd like to sit down and tell her so, but if she was going to run, so was he. She sprinted on and he followed until the plane was finally in sight. It looked fine.

"Get in and fly this thing!" she yelled as she climbed up.

He mentally ran down the list to see if there was anything in the preflight checklist that couldn't wait.

Another shot fired.

No. Everything could wait.

He climbed in and did as she said, taking off more roughly than he had since he'd first started flying.

But they were up and in minutes would be out of range. For now.

Will focused on the instrument panel, clenching and unclenching his fists on the wheel to try to calm his nerves. When he was sure they were safe, he turned to McKenna. "What were you thinking? You should have gotten down!"

"I knew what I was doing."

"You almost got us killed. You're new at this, McKenna." He let the frustration of the past however many hours loose in his tone.

"I'm new to the area not to the job. I've been doing this for years, and I really do know what I'm doing. It's my job, Will. Not yours."

"I have experience, life experience you don't have."

"Five years more, Will. That's it. I'm not a kid."

"I still wish you'd listened to me."

"This is my *job,* Will. I have to make split-second judgments and not look back. But I am trained to do it. And if we're going to be working together, you're going to have to trust me to know the right course instead of second-guessing me."

Will took a deep breath, powering down emotions that had gone wild at the thought of her being hurt or killed. Yeah, this was her job. Theoretically she had the necessary training for it. But that stupid running-to-the-plane stunt while they were taking fire...

"Okay." He could think of nothing else to say.

"Couldn't you hear that the shots were fired from closer range the second time?"

He hadn't noticed that. "You're sure?"

She nodded, face more serious than he'd ever seen it. "I'm sure."

So the shooter had been creeping closer the whole time they'd been waiting him out, hoping he'd leave. That made sense since his first couple shots hadn't hit his mark.

"I guess I owe you an apology then."

"No need. You saved my life the first time by taking me down with you."

He nodded, knowing she was right. But she'd saved his life, too, by insisting that they run for the plane. This time, their shared skills and experience had been enough to keep them safe. But the shooter wasn't someone to underestimate, and he'd almost certainly strike again. Will just hoped his own abilities and McKenna's would be enough to protect them through the next skirmish, too.

Will hadn't said another word until they'd reached Barrow, landed the plane and were unloading.

"Be careful, McKenna," he finally said. His eyes met hers and the intensity in them made it impossible for her to look away.

"I will be. I can take care—"

"Of yourself. You've made that clear."

She couldn't read what emotion was in his eyes. Couldn't come close to naming it. But whatever it was stirred something inside of her, and maybe it was that, or the stress of the day, but she couldn't picture going home with no human company. Not yet.

"Want to come over for coffee?"

He glanced at his watch. "It's five-thirty and you're more worried about coffee than dinner?"

McKenna shrugged, feeling herself blush. She hadn't

even thought about what time it was, had just come up with any reason she could to spend a little more time with Will.

"How about I fix dinner for us and then we'll have coffee, maybe watch a movie," he offered.

She searched his face for any indication that he was doing this out of pity for her, or that he knew she was scared, but saw none.

He must have misinterpreted her silence, because he hurried to clarify. "Not as a date or anything. Just two old friends, hanging out, if that's what you're worried about." His easy smile, meant to reassure her, made a blush creep to the edges of her cheeks.

For a split second, she squeezed her eyes shut. Imagined what it would be like to actually be on a *date* with Will Harrison. Then just as quickly she shoved the thought back where it had come from. The last thing she needed was to get caught thinking such embarrassing things about someone who was only her friend.

"I thought you couldn't cook?" she said as soon as she remembered.

The corners of his eyes crinkled as he laughed. "By fix dinner I meant bring pizza."

"Is there a pizza place in this town?" She didn't remember seeing one. But she hadn't been everywhere yet.

"Bear's Tooth Pub and Pizzeria is as good or better than anything you'll find in the city. They have a deluxe pizza that's unbelievably good. I'll swing by your house as soon as I pick it up. Sound good?"

"Works for me. But don't pile up the pizza under loads of stuff. I want to be able to taste the cheese."

"Trust me, will you? I promise you'll like it."

His words still rang in her ears as she climbed into her car and drove toward her house. She did trust him. With her life. She just knew better than to ever again trust him with her heart.

She parked her car on the gravel pad beside her house and climbed the stairs to the front door with caution, looking around to make sure nothing had been disturbed while she was gone. She eased the door open and Mollie came barreling toward her, tongue hanging out of her mouth.

"I'm guessing you missed me?" McKenna laughed as she petted the dog and pulled the door shut behind her. "I would have brought you if I hadn't been afraid you'd attract wild animals I would rather not run into."

The dog just wagged her tail and continued to dance around excitedly.

"Will's coming over tonight," she found herself telling the dog. "To hang out with me." In case that part needed clarification. It was strange to her to think that after all these years they'd picked up their friendship practically where they'd left off, ignoring the awkwardness that had started between them just before Will left for college when she'd come close to fully admitting the childish crush she had on him.

Of course, a lot had changed since then. When Will had left Seward, McKenna had wanted to become a marine biologist and work at the Sealife Center in Seward. Now look what she was doing. Will hadn't been sure what he'd wanted to do when he headed off to college, but he'd gotten married and started on his adult life.

Now, seven years later, here they were.

McKenna shoved her reminiscences aside. It would be better to use the time she had to go over the case.

As she walked by the kitchen table, she glanced at the spot where she'd first spotted the threatening note. It was still there. She kept walking and then stopped in her tracks, walking backward as she blinked quickly, in case her eyes had deceived her. Hadn't she moved it?

No, a paper was there. But it wasn't the note that she'd found in the early hours of the morning. This one was new.

He'd been in her house. Again.

You chose not to listen. Suit yourself. I may have missed this time, but next time will be a different story.

FOUR

The text he'd gotten from McKenna had said come quick. Which was why Will was barreling down the narrow dirt road to her house. He couldn't think of any good reason she'd text him that, but plenty of bad ones came to mind.

He pressed the gas a little harder and swung the truck into her pitiful excuse for a driveway. What she'd been thinking when she rented this place, he'd never understand. He knew troopers weren't rich, but they were paid enough to afford better than this.

"McKenna?" he yelled as he took the steps two at a time and tried the doorknob. It was locked. He pounded on the door, not caring what the neighbors might be thinking. "McKenna!"

When she finally opened the door, Will's eyebrows rose. She'd kept her cool throughout the scene earlier in the day when they'd been shot at by a sniper, but now her eyes were wide and her face had paled several shades lighter than normal. Her dog stood next to her, looking tense.

"He was here," McKenna whispered.

"Where?"

She gulped. "In my house." Hands quivering, she held out a piece of paper that Will took and read. He wanted to ball it up in his fist—what kind of person threatened another like that?—but he knew it was evidence. Valuable evidence. "Is this all you found?"

"Yes."

"Did you check the rest of the house? To make sure nothing's out of place?"

"Of course." She flashed him a look of annoyance. "I cleared all of the rooms and then sat down on the couch with Mollie."

"You're not staying here anymore."

He watched her features harden and her eyes begin to flash. "I don't know why you think you have the right to make my choices for me, but it's my decision." She lifted her chin, challenging him to respond.

Will did what he'd learned was best to do when McKenna's Irish temper flared and her safety was at stake. He ignored it. "This place is a dump. You shouldn't have been living here in the first place."

"The price was good."

"Are you saying this is all you can afford? Is it legal for the state to pay troopers that little?"

She moved toward him and reopened the front door. "Thanks for coming. I changed my mind. I'll figure this out on my own."

"Look." Will pushed the door closed. "We're friends, McKenna. You're like a sister to me and I'm just trying to help you. Now, seriously, do you have the money for a better place? I can help you out with that if you need it." He knew she wouldn't take the offer but figured he'd put it out there for what it was worth. He'd meant what he said, her family had given him a second home during high school, years he hadn't wanted to be at his house. Taking care of her now was the least he could do.

"I make plenty," she insisted, collapsing back into her seat on the sofa. "But…" She shrugged. "I'm hoping this job won't last long, so I'm saving my pay to get a nice place when I move again."

Will had expected as much—she'd all but said she didn't want to be in a town like Barrow when he'd talked her into taking him on as her pilot, but it still hurt to hear her admit that this town wasn't worth it to her.

"Maybe if you solve this case they'll be so impressed they'll promote you again."

McKenna laughed. "Yeah, straight to somewhere like Dutch Harbor," she joked, naming a town about the size of Barrow that sat almost at the end of the Aleutian Island chain. "Not exactly the step up I'd be hoping for, but with my luck…"

"How about you solve it anyway, just to put my mind at ease, okay?"

Her face sobered. "I'm sorry again about today, Will. I never guessed all of that would happen. I hate that I put you in that situation."

"I'm glad I was there with you, even if I wasn't really much help."

A few heartbeats of silence passed. McKenna's piercing gaze never left his. He shifted in his seat, still not comfortable that all was clear. Or maybe that was just discomfort over how close they'd ended up sitting. "Let's check the rest of the house one more time. In more detail," Will said at last, finally breaking their eye contact. If they sat there too long, it felt as if she'd be able to see straight to the center of his heart. And he wasn't ready to let *anyone* that close. Not again.

To his surprise, she didn't fight him. Just nodded and stood.

Together they searched the bathroom and McKenna's bedroom. Everything was clear. Will's mind was telling him to relax, but his body wouldn't obey. Something still had his shoulders tense.

"It's clear," she insisted again. "Nothing but that note on the table."

"Remind me what that said again?" Will requested as he checked the hall closet for a third time. He couldn't shake the feeling they were overlooking something.

"Something about how he might have missed that time, but he wouldn't the next time," she recounted again, her face twisting in distaste at the words.

He couldn't blame her. The guy, whoever was behind this, had certainly made his intentions clear.

Maybe that was why Will felt as if he couldn't let his guard back down. Maybe there was nothing in the house right now that could pose a threat, just the general threat that the man was still out there.

"Where's Mollie?" He'd only just noticed she wasn't with them. She'd followed them from the living room at the start of their search and had been faithfully nosing around behind them. Will had watched her lift her snout to sniff the air a few times, as if she thought she could help that way, but even her best attempts hadn't uncovered anything. She'd seemed extra needy for attention as they'd continued searching, but then had disappeared.

McKenna looked around. "She was just here, wasn't she?" Alarm crept into her tone.

They retraced their steps around the small house until they found Mollie stretched out on the floor in McKenna's room. "You okay, girl?" McKenna knelt down next to the dog, who sleepily raised her head to meet her owner's gaze, then flopped back onto the floor.

The eyes McKenna turned on Will were full of panic. "You don't think…"

He watched the dog for a minute, seeing what McKenna

saw even after the limited exposure he'd had to Mollie. The dog wasn't herself.

"You don't think they poisoned her?" McKenna finally asked, the words trailing to a whisper at the end of her question, as if she'd had to force herself to ask.

Poisoning the dog after sneaking into the house undetected didn't make sense. If someone were going to hurt Mollie, they would have done it already. But that didn't explain her strange behavior. Will watched her again, thought back on her behavior since he'd arrived. She'd seemed fine initially, then sniffed around as if she was helping them search....

He pictured her with her nose in the air sniffing. What if she hadn't been searching for an intruder's scent, as he'd initially thought? What if she'd smelled something wrong? Was that why she'd tried to get their attention?

Will sniffed the air himself, finally catching hints of an odor like rotten eggs that triggered alarm bells in his mind.

He scooped the dog in his arms. "Gas leak!" he called back to McKenna as he hurried out into the hallway. "Get out. Follow me!"

He glanced behind him once to make sure McKenna had listened.

"I'm here! Keep going, get her out!" she yelled.

They burst through the front door, leaving it standing open. For a few seconds they just stood there, staring at the house. Then Will dialed the fire department's emergency number.

The North Slope Bureau Fire Department truck pulled in front of the house within ten minutes. "You said it's a gas leak?" a firefighter confirmed as he stepped out of the truck.

"Yes." Will cast a glance at the dog, who seemed to be

recovering from the effects of inhaling the gas. He stole a look at McKenna's face, too. Her eyes looked haunted.

"Gotcha." The man went back to what he was doing. "These things can be dangerous. Lucky no one was hurt."

Will didn't know if he should warn the man that they suspected the gas line had been cut on purpose, but decided after a few seconds that it wouldn't change how he handled the scene. And anyway, Will wasn't sure who they could trust. He turned to McKenna, hoping she was ready to be reasonable about her living situation.

"I have a friend at the hunting service where I work. His sister-in-law mentioned she was thinking of looking for a roommate. Her name's Anna Richmond and I think we should call her."

McKenna nodded, eyes darting to Mollie even as she reached to stroke her fur. "I agree. I'm not going to risk her getting hurt again."

What about you? he wanted to ask her. But he didn't see any reason to remind her of the number of near-death experiences she'd had during the course of twenty-four hours.

Unfortunately, today had taught them both a lesson. Whoever was behind this was serious. He wouldn't stop until he was sure McKenna was out of his way.

"You had a gas leak for sure." The firefighter had reported, face grim. "I've got the gas shut off, but the gas line needs to be repaired as soon as possible. You should be thankful the whole house didn't—" He looked at McKenna and cleared his throat, like the rest of the words were stuck there.

"Go kaboom?" she finished for him. She turned to Will. "I guess this means we'll have to take a rain check on watching a movie" was all McKenna could find to say.

"Looks like. But we can eat pizza in the car on the

way to Anna's house." He'd stepped aside to call Anna, and returned with assurances that the other woman was looking forward to her arrival. They climbed into Will's truck, McKenna second-guessing her decision to stay with a stranger a little more with every passing moment.

This whole plan made McKenna uncomfortable. "Are you sure she won't mind a total stranger living with her?"

"I'm sure."

He sounded confident, as if he knew Anna well. McKenna's stomach clenched. Were he and Anna a couple? She'd assumed this whole time that Will was single, as he had been since his wife had died so young. Not that it mattered…or *should* matter. Because it shouldn't.

She let a few minutes of silence pass, hoping her curiosity would fizzle naturally.

It didn't.

"You sound like you know her well," McKenna began. "Are you…"

Will looked away from the road long enough to raise his eyebrows and shake his head. "Dating? No."

She wanted to ask why, her curiosity kindled even more by his abrupt reply. Although she suspected she already know the answer—Rachael, his late wife, had been a vibrant, beautiful woman. It would be hard for anyone to measure up to the invisible standard Will must be carrying around.

She didn't want to think about why that thought fell over her like clouds covering the sun. McKenna focused on her dog, who was curled up on the floorboards at her feet. She reached down to pet her.

"So we're going to try to move all my stuff tonight?" she asked to try to distract herself from the unpleasant might-have-beens that kept threatening to overwhelm her imagination.

"I think that's wise. I don't want you going back there. What if he'd been waiting outside when you opened the door tonight?"

She'd thought of that already. McKenna suppressed a shiver.

"Or worse," he continued, "what if, instead of cutting the gas line, he'd decided to hide in a closet or something to wait until you were inside with the door locked to attack you?"

"He probably couldn't have done that without Mollie giving him away." She reasoned.

He frowned in her direction. "I don't like this at all, McKenna. Why is he pursuing you so seriously?"

"Because I found his crime scene?"

He nodded. "Yeah…but what does he gain by attacking you? The troopers would just send in someone else to investigate. It's almost like it's getting personal with him."

"What do you mean?"

Will shrugged. "Call it a feeling more than anything. You can't think of anyone you know who might be behind this, can you?"

"Not unless they followed me from Anchorage. I'm new here, remember? Maybe the pilot the troopers were using before…but I don't have any evidence against him. It's just a feeling." Nothing more was said, since they pulled up in front of a house that McKenna assumed must be Anna's.

"This is it." Will motioned in front of them with his hand. "It's nothing fancy, but it's nicer than your old place. Better part of town, too. And—" he pointed to another house within sight range "—my friend Matt and his wife, Lexi, live right there."

Uneasiness swirled in McKenna's stomach. Being reminded that these were people Will knew and cared about made her hesitant to move in. What if her presence put them in danger?

"You're not worried about your friends being close to me when I'm obviously a target?"

"You're my friend."

"I know that. But what about the others?"

"I'd do anything to keep you safe, McKenna. Don't you get that? Matt, Lexi and Anna all know what they're getting into, anyway. And they're used to danger. There was quite a bit of that involved in Matt and Lexi's lives right when they met and started dating, from what they've told me."

She nodded slowly. "If you're really sure—and if they are, too."

"Everybody's sure."

"I guess this is it, then." McKenna reached for the door handle. "And you did tell her I have a dog?"

Mollie's head lifted, as though she knew she was being talked about. Will reached down to pet her. "Like I'd forget you, girl. Yes, McKenna. And she doesn't care, she has one, too. Everything has been taken care of and is going to be fine."

He seemed confident. She could hear it in his tone. She could only hope he was right and that he had enough faith for both of them.

McKenna knocked on the front door, making an effort to stand straight, which was more difficult than usual since she could feel the stress of the past forty-eight hours weighing on her.

The door opened and a petite blonde smiled before stepping forward and wrapping McKenna in a hug. "You must be McKenna! I'm so glad to have you here. I'm Anna Richmond."

"Nice to meet you, Anna." McKenna managed to remember the manners her mom had taught her, despite her surprise at getting such a warm reception. "I appreciate your letting me live here."

"You're doing me a favor," she said with a smile as she released McKenna. "Checkers is good company, but he doesn't talk back, you know?" She motioned to a dog that looked like a mix between a border collie and a terrier.

"I understand." McKenna reached down and petted Mollie between the ears. "This is Mollie."

The two dogs were nose to nose, sniffing each other cautiously, and then ran inside the house together.

"I think they're going to get along fine," Anna said with confidence. "Now, let's get you moved in. What can I help with?"

They walked to the car and the three of them brought in McKenna's things. Thankfully, she'd anticipated having less space in Barrow and had left a lot of her possessions in storage in Anchorage. The dumpy trailer she'd rented had come furnished, so she hadn't needed much. It made moving into Anna's house much easier. Will only had to make one more trip to her old house and back, one he insisted on making alone, to pick up the last of her belongings.

Over an hour later, McKenna sank into one of the chairs in the living room. "What time is it?" she asked, looking around for a clock. It was still light outside, but in September that didn't tell her much. "I'm ready for bed."

Will checked his watch and laughed. "It's almost nine."

McKenna tried to stifle a yawn. "You've got to be kidding."

"You have had kind of a long day," Anna offered.

Had they really only been shot at that morning? "I guess if you don't mind, I'm going to turn in early."

Will stood as McKenna did. "I'm going to head over to Matt's and say hi before I go home." He started toward the door, then paused and faced McKenna. "Be careful, okay? I'll see you tomorrow."

He'd insisted on keeping her company the next day, "just in case she needed him for anything," he'd said. She knew he was concerned about whoever was after her and felt as if he needed to look out for her. To be honest, she thought it was overkill. Moving in with Anna had ensured that she wouldn't be alone at night anymore, which seemed like the most vulnerable time. During the day? Well, she had a gun and she knew how to use it. Personally, she thought Will should go back to work, but if she knew him at all, she knew he was stubborn—almost as stubborn as she was—and she knew telling him to do anything would be useless.

Besides, it was a little sweet that he cared.

FIVE

Will knocked on his friend's door, willing himself not to shiver in the cold that crept through his jacket.

"Hey!" Matt greeted when he opened the door. "Did you get her all settled in?"

He nodded. "Yep. She and Anna seem to get along fine, so that's good, too. It was nice of her to let McKenna move in."

"It didn't sound like a good situation, living alone where she was."

Once again, Will marveled at the independence—or was it stubbornness?—McKenna continued to show. She was no longer technically a kid, but she was still young, still needed taking care of.

"You okay? You seem distracted," Matt asked as Will followed him inside. The whole house smelled like warm cinnamon.

"I am a little. But it's nothing that a little of whatever I smell couldn't cure." He looked around and found the source of the aroma—several pans of cinnamon rolls—sitting on a kitchen counter.

"Help yourself," Lexi said with a smile as she pulled another pan out of the oven. "There are plenty." She handed him a small plate and put a warm cinnamon roll on it.

"Thanks." He picked up a fork and after one bite, closed his eyes and smiled. "This is epic." He looked at Matt. "How you don't weigh five-hundred pounds is a mystery to all of us."

Matt laughed. "She is an amazing cook. I highly recommend this whole marriage thing."

Will swallowed hard in the sudden silence. Lexi fixed her husband with a look.

"I'm sorry, man. I didn't mean—" Matt started.

"It's okay," Will said.

"It has been a long time, Will. Maybe it is time for you to think about dating again." Lexi said it gently, with a smile. "Tell me about your friend."

"Who? McKenna?"

"Like there are other women I could be talking about?"

Some part of him had a hard time thinking of McKenna as a *woman*. Clearly she'd grown up and wasn't the girl he remembered. But *woman* made her seem…

Lexi had a point, though. Who else would she be talking about? He had made a very concentrated effort to avoid getting involved with anyone since he came to town. It wasn't too difficult since women were scarce in the area anyway. But he wasn't ready for another relationship. He wasn't sure his heart had recovered from the last one.

He said as much to Lexi, who just waved him off. "It's been, what, five years since you came here? So you've had a long enough time, I would think."

"Maybe you're right." Will shrugged. "I've never done this before—thought about dating after being married."

"So, you are thinking about dating her?" Lexi, ever the matchmaker, rubbed her hands together.

Great. That hadn't come out the way he'd meant. "No. She's my best friend's little sister." He shifted uncomfortably, knowing there was more to it than that. McKenna was the kind of woman who would engage every emotion—which would only make it even easier to get his heart thoroughly shattered if something ever happened to her, the way something had happened to Rachael. He was better off single. "Hey, can I have another cinnamon roll?"

Lexi pushed the pan toward him but maintained a steady stare. She clearly wasn't letting him get away with the change in subject.

Surely someone could use this woman's persistence in an interrogation room somewhere. "Matt, do you want to help me out here?" he called to his friend, who was sitting on the couch in the living room, and listening to the whole conversation with what seemed like great amusement.

"Nah, you're doing great on your own."

Will turned back to Lexi the inquisitor. "You should stick to baking rather than matchmaking. You're much better at it."

She raised her eyebrows. "I didn't say anything. You brought the subject back up, technically, which makes me think you really are interested." She folded her arms and narrowed her eyes. "The question is, why aren't you doing something about it?"

Will set his fork down. "Even *if* I was interested. And that's something I'm not saying, by the way. *If* I was, she's still my best friend's sister." And there was that host of other reasons, too....

"So?"

Matt laughed louder.

"I'm glad you're enjoying this," Will called over his shoulder.

"Oh, I am."

"It's just not something guys do," Will tried to explain. "Sisters are off-limits."

"Because that makes sense. She's an adult, Will. Really

pretty, too. I looked out the window while you guys were moving her stuff in."

"Look, she's off-limits, guys. Leave it alone."

Out of the corner of his eye he saw Matt and Lexi exchange a look. They might not believe him, but he was sure of it—nothing beyond friendship could ever happen between him and McKenna Clark.

Nothing had broken all day on the case McKenna had been working so hard on. Of course, part of the problem was that no matter how hard she worked, she couldn't give the case her full attention.

She'd learned even in the past eight hours how difficult it was to multitask when you had no coworkers to rely on for support. In Anchorage, if she'd had a case this critical, someone else would have taken the other duties she held and taken care of things like the moose that had mysteriously dropped dead too close to town and was attracting wolves. Unfortunately, he hadn't been discovered until the meat had gone bad, so McKenna hadn't been able to give the meat to anyone. She'd just had to load it up in the back of an old pickup and drive it farther from town where the wolves wouldn't pose a threat to townspeople.

There hadn't been any need for Will to go with her, since she hadn't needed the use of a plane, so she'd sent him a text that morning to let him know she'd be fine for the day on her own.

It was funny how much she wished she'd let him tag along with her, just to provide an extra set of eyes and some company.

But this wasn't Will's job; it was hers. And she wanted to prove she could do it well.

McKenna walked up the steps to her and Anna's house. She put her key in the door and opened it only to be greeted by Mollie, Checkers and the mess they'd made while she and Anna had been working.

"So you were into the tissues today, huh?" she noted as she locked the door behind her and put her bag down by the door. The living room was covered in little piles of tissues that looked almost like the snow McKenna knew would soon be blanketing the landscape outside. "Looks exciting."

There was a bump outside, around the back of the house. McKenna tilted her head to listen but didn't hear anything else. Feeling as if she was probably just being paranoid, she hurried to the bathroom, where the window would give her a view in that direction, and looked out.

Nothing.

She was starting to jump at shadows. The anxiety from this case was building, she could feel it in the tensing of her shoulders and the fact that her racing heart never quite seemed to calm down.

She'd had a call from Captain Wilkins earlier in the day, checking on her progress.

"It's just…stalled," she'd confessed, not knowing what else to say.

"That needs to change. We have enough trouble in your bureau with poachers. We don't need an unsolved double murder, too."

At his words *unsolved double murder,* she'd shivered. After she'd finished talking to him, she'd called the medical examiner's office in Anchorage where the bodies had been taken. Though tox screens and all the other details usually took a few weeks to be finished, she'd hoped they'd have information for her already. Unfortunately, the person she talked to had informed her that not only was there nothing to tell yet, but also that even though they could release information to her since she was official law enforcement, it would have to be in person.

McKenna wondered how Will would feel about flying her to Anchorage in the next few weeks.

Jerking back to the present, McKenna tensed as she heard someone jangle the doorknob, then relaxed as Anna's voiced called, "I'm home, did you miss me?"

McKenna laughed. "I did, actually."

"This roommate thing is kinda nice so far." Anna smiled. "Much less lonely. So. Any ideas for dinner? I'm starving."

"Will offered to bring pizza." McKenna had gotten a text from him just as she was leaving work and hadn't texted back yet.

"Ooh, tell him yes. Pizza sounds great."

McKenna texted Will, who said he'd be over soon. True to his word, he was knocking on the door ten minutes later.

"You managed to get a pizza ordered and picked up in ten minutes?" McKenna asked as she opened the door for him.

Will shook his head and grinned. "Nah. I'd already ordered it. I had a feeling you'd say yes."

"Did you?"

"Yeah. You've missed me today."

McKenna laughed. "Have I?"

He shrugged. "You may not admit it, but I know the truth."

Their eyes locked and something fluttered inside McKenna. She swallowed it down. He was just teasing her, he'd probably consider it *brotherly* teasing. She didn't need to read more into it than was there.

"Is that Will with the food?" Anna called from the kitchen.

McKenna tore her gaze away from Will's. "Yeah." She

looked at him one last time and then turned away. "He's here."

She walked to the kitchen, Will following her. They set out the food and began to eat.

"So, nothing unusual has happened? You're both feeling safe?" Will asked, concern lacing his tone.

Anna laughed. "Are you kidding? My roomie's a state trooper. I feel completely safe."

"How about you?" He turned to McKenna.

She nodded. "I have a gun, so I'm good. And it's nice knowing Lexi and Matt are close. I'm guessing they could come to our rescue, too."

"Well, not with a gun," Anna corrected her. "But yeah, they'd be there if we needed them."

McKenna frowned. "I thought everyone had a gun up here, either for safety or hunting."

Anna's gaze darted to Will, then back at McKenna. She shrugged and looked back to Will.

"I didn't want to say anything because I didn't want it to cloud your opinion of him…." Will began. Uh-oh. Nothing good ever started that way.

"But?" McKenna asked, her stomach suddenly not in the mood for pizza, or any other food, as she wondered what Will could be leading up to.

"Matt has a criminal record. The particular offense that restricts him from having a gun was actually more an incident of being in the wrong place at the wrong time, but he's not allowed to own one anyway."

Something cold curled in the pit of McKenna's stomach. Will had made it clear that being here with Anna would be good partially because her sister and brother-in-law lived so close and could keep an eye on them, help keep them safe. After everything that had happened, Will had asked her to entrust her safety to a convicted felon?

Had he lost his mind?

That was exactly what she asked with the look she gave him, but his eyes warned her not to ask the question out loud. Either he was worried about offending Anna, since Matt was family, or he really believed Matt was a good guy. Maybe both.

Regardless, McKenna couldn't believe he expected her to accept that for herself without proof. She was working a murder case, and he had just told her that there was someone very close at hand who could be considered a suspect.

She looked over at Anna, who was eating her pizza, conscientiously keeping her eyes on her plate, as if she was trying not to interrupt the private fight McKenna and Will were having silently.

"Oh," McKenna finally said. "I didn't know." She grasped for something to change the subject, lighten the mood. "So, does anyone want to watch a movie after dinner?"

Anna and Will both jumped at it.

As Anna went to pick a movie and Will helped her clean up the kitchen, McKenna's mind stayed on the new revelation that Matt had a criminal past. Whether or not it would offend Anna and Will, McKenna was going to have to look into this. It was her case and she had to do as thorough a job as possible. People's lives, *her* life, could depend on it.

Will had finally left just before midnight, and McKenna had gone straight to bed. The events of the week and the revelations from that night weighed heavily on her mind. She was sure they would keep her awake, and yet she was asleep almost the moment she hit the pillow.

"McKenna."

In her dream, someone was shaking her. Or maybe it

was an earthquake. It was hard to tell with dreams. And it was almost like someone was calling her....

"McKenna!"

She blinked her eyes open and saw Anna standing beside the bed, fully dressed. She sat up, scooting back against the pillow and willing herself awake. "What's wrong?" A quick glance of the bedroom showed nothing out of place, and she couldn't hear anything out of the ordinary, but it felt like the middle of the night and she didn't know why Anna would be up.

"We're fine. But I just got a call in to work. There's a body on the beach just outside of town. It doesn't look as if he died of natural causes, according to my supervisor. Since I'm on call, I'll be one of the paramedics responsible for handling the body until it can be flown to the M.E.'s office in Anchorage. I don't know any details yet, but wondered if you wanted to come, just in case it's connected to your case somehow."

McKenna was already pulling a sweatshirt on over her pajama shirt. "Give me a second to change. I'll be right there."

Anna left the room and McKenna changed into jeans and put shoes on in record time.

Mollie looked up with mild interest as she exited. "Go back to sleep, girl," McKenna told her and the dog lay back down, seemingly relieved that she didn't have to interrupt her dreams.

"We'll have to take the ATVs. The crime scene is past the roads."

McKenna nodded, having anticipated this. There were no roads from Barrow to another town, so if you needed to get anywhere outside of town, you had to take an all-terrain vehicle or fly.

They each jumped on their four-wheelers and Anna led the way to the place she'd been told to go.

Several emergency personnel had already gathered and the lights they'd set up around the crime scene cast a hazy orange glow on the otherwise-dark night.

And it *was* a crime scene. That had taken McKenna no time to realize. The pool of blood under the man and the wound she could see looked consistent with a gunshot.

In fact, the entire scene looked eerily familiar.

Her throat tightened and she fought to take even breaths. Frustration warred with the panic that was building—she needed to be able to handle this. Captain Wilkins was right—she had the training, the tools needed to solve this case. She just needed to pull herself together and do it.

"Thanks for bringing me," McKenna whispered to Anna.

"So it's connected to your case?" Anna looked pleased that she'd been able to help.

"I'm pretty sure." McKenna looked around the dark expanse of rugged shoreline. The wind from the Arctic Ocean stabbed through her clothes, even with the coat she'd grabbed on her way out the door. She shivered.

Anna walked toward the other emergency personnel.

McKenna did her best to stay out of the way, since this wasn't her crime scene. Anna and the other paramedic, who had apparently arrived just minutes before her, were examining the body, and a man from the North Slope Bureau Police Department stood nearby.

"Looks like he hasn't been gone long." Anna shook her head.

"Even if someone had found him sooner," the other paramedic began, "blood loss would have been too great."

An even greater heaviness seemed to descend on the scene. McKenna wandered to the edge of the lit-up area and scanned the darkness that surrounded them. Nothing seemed out of place. In fact, everything seemed peaceful and utterly quiet. Too quiet for her taste, since it left nothing to distract her from the clamorous thoughts in her mind.

Why would someone shoot a man this far out of town and leave him there?

Or maybe the better question was, what was he doing so far out of town that ended up getting him shot?

This wasn't like some of the cases she'd heard about at the trooper academy, where people got in fights and killed each other in the heat of the moment. Cases like that were all too common in the Alaskan bush because of the rampant alcohol abuse. No, this was different. This was planned, in a location where there would be no witnesses.

She could see no signs of a struggle from where she stood. She assumed there might have been tracks of some kind that could have been investigated, but those would have been compromised when the first paramedic responded to the scene. She didn't fault them for not preserving the integrity of the area—the possibility that they could save a life had to come first.

She pulled out a notebook she'd been using to jot down thoughts about the case, and recorded everything she saw, including impressions about the man, from what she could see of him. He was dressed in hunting camo.

"Who called this in?" McKenna asked when Anna came near her again.

She pointed to a man who looked to be a civilian. "That guy over there. His name is George. He's one of Barrow's most vocal residents. Have you met him yet?"

McKenna noted Anna's raised eyebrows, and her own raised in curiosity for what could cause her to have that reaction to the man. "No, I haven't."

"Talking to him might be a good place to start. Just… don't let him get to you. He can be kind of abrasive."

McKenna made her way to where the man stood. He was Native Alaskan and was one of those people who seemed to defy the ability to pinpoint age. She'd guess him to be in his early fifties, but knew she could be off by twenty years either way. "Excuse me, sir?" she said to get his attention as she approached.

He met her gaze and the expression in his eyes shifted from disinterest in the scene around him to unmistakable contempt. "What do you want?"

"I have a couple of questions about how you found this man here."

"You're the new wildlife trooper, aren't you?"

"I am. I'm McKenna Clark."

He looked at her outstretched hand but didn't reach for it. "That man, he isn't wildlife. So why do you care?"

"I care because I'm concerned he may be related to another case I'm working on."

The man smirked. "Ah."

His knowing smile made her uneasy. He couldn't know about that case, could he? The details of it had been kept quiet. Since those murders had occurred so far out of town, no one could know about them. Could they?

She cleared her throat, hoping he'd give her some details that could help. "So, could you tell me how you found him? What were you doing out this way?"

"Wildlife troopers are just in the way up here. I hope you know that. You mess with the native way of life. The government has no business telling us how or when we can hunt."

So much for getting his cooperation.

"Could you answer the question, please?" she asked

firmly, hoping she'd mostly kept the irritation she could feel rising in her throat out of her tone of voice.

"All the government has brought here are too many rules, too many regulations and too many men who care nothing for the land or the animals and use them for their own gain. We need to protect our land from the government and from his kind." He jerked his head in the direction of the dead man. "Not the other way around."

So, that was a no, then—he wouldn't be answering her question, or helping her in any way. "I guess you're not up for questions." She sighed and turned away, walking closer to where the paramedics were now loading the dead man into a medevac helicopter. Then she froze. *His kind?* What had George meant by that?

She turned around to ask him, but he was gone. Either he'd lost himself in the cluster of emergency personnel—not likely since there were only three of them—or he'd wandered far enough away to not be illuminated by the lights.

Something told her he knew more than he was saying. So the question was, could he be a valuable asset to helping her solve the murders?

Or was he the one behind them?

Will was just leaving for work when he got an SOS text from McKenna telling him the coffeemaker at the trooper post was broken and asking if he could bring her some. He checked his watch. He'd planned to leave early just because he'd woken up early, but he didn't need to be at work for over an hour. This would provide a good excuse to make sure she hadn't had any more threats or close calls she hadn't told him about, before he got to work and prepared for his afternoon hunt.

He made the coffee and texted her back that he was

coming, to which she'd replied Thanks. I've been up almost all night.

That had made him pick up the pace even more. Had there been a new lead on the case? He'd barely put his truck in Park before he got out and ran to pound on the door of McKenna's office.

"Hi! I found out some information on the man who was shot on the beach." McKenna's eyes glittered with excitement. "Are you ready?"

"Whoa." He held the coffee mug and carafe away from her. "You sound like you're caffeinated enough."

"Not a drop yet today, mister. Give me that coffee and nobody gets hurt."

He handed it to her and she poured herself a mug, took a long sip and smiled. "Ah. I can think better now. Okay. Ready?"

"First, what man on the beach?"

"I forgot, you didn't know." She took a deep breath and filled him in on the previous night's events. He could picture her, silhouetted by the glow of the lights the investigators and paramedics would have been using, while a killer was out there and after her. It wasn't a picture he liked, but if it had produced a lead, maybe he should try not to think about it. "Should I be sitting down for this?" he asked.

She seemed to consider it. "Nah. It's exciting, but not game changing."

"Okay. Go ahead."

"His name is Seth Davison."

"Never heard of him."

"Exactly. That's because he wasn't a local. We talked to his family and found out he was here on a hunting trip."

Will shook his head. "I don't see how that's a lead. Just about everyone who comes here is here to hunt."

"You're probably right. But it's still something to look

into. Especially since the other two victims were here to hunt, too. There has to be a connection."

"So where will you start?"

"Investigating the hunting-guide companies around here. Starting today with your competition. Tomorrow I'll be at Truman."

Rick was going to love that. Much as Will wanted her to do whatever it took to solve the case, even if it made people uncomfortable, he knew her inquiry into Rick's business wasn't going to make his boss easy to handle.

"My boss is not going to like that."

McKenna laughed. "Of course he's not going to like it. No one likes being investigated for anything. But I've got to follow up on this, just in case."

"You're right." And she was. But he'd rather be anywhere but Barrow when Rick found out he was being investigated. He was a decent boss and usually an easygoing guy—but stress brought out the worst in anybody.

"What do you think?" She studied him, insecurity flickering in her eyes. McKenna, insecure? He wouldn't have guessed it. Will had known her since she was born but he had a feeling he could know her for years more and not *really* know everything about her. She was more intriguing, more complex, than anyone he'd ever known.

"I think it's a good idea to investigate any possible lead you can."

"But you don't think it's going to turn up anything."

"Not really."

"Because you trust your boss that much?"

"Not that, I just don't know why you'd suspect the hunting agencies. Just because the victims came to hunt doesn't mean they were with a company. Maybe they planned to hunt with local friends, or hire a pilot."

"But you do see that hunting is connected somehow."

"I see how it *seems* connected. What do they call that—circumstantial evidence?"

She leveled him with a glare, took a long sip of coffee. "Humor me for a minute here. Or do you have to go?"

Will glanced at his watch. Still half an hour to spare. He looked around the room and his eyes settled on a metal folding chair propped against one of the walls. He grabbed it, opened it and sat. "Go ahead, I'm all yours." He cringed when the words came out. He hadn't meant them that way.

But if McKenna noticed how…awkwardly they could be taken, she didn't say. She just went on.

"I'm assuming the deaths on the tundra and the body on the beach are connected somehow. The scenes felt very similar, and all the victims came to this area to hunt. Still with me?"

"Yeah, I see where you're going. Hunting is coming up everywhere."

"Exactly."

"Handy, since you're a wildlife trooper."

McKenna grinned. "Ha-ha." Then her face fell. "But beyond that, I'm just guessing. I'm going to investigate the hunting companies, see if anyone has heard of any of the three victims and just check for anything questionable in general in how those companies are operated."

"Maybe…"

"What?"

Will leaned forward, elbows on his knees, to meet McKenna's eyes. "I'm no trooper, but I am a hunter. Maybe I can help you brainstorm, try to help you understand what could have gone on. I've got a lot of experience with the people who come out here to hunt. The guys I take on trips with me usually have a certain personality type—maybe understanding that could help in some way."

She seemed to consider his proposal, then nodded, and he let out a breath he hadn't realized he'd held.

"Now," he began, "you have to realize this is just a general picture. I don't know if your dead guys fit this or not."

"Speculation could help my mind figure something out, so I'll take what I can get."

"Okay. The hunters who come here are almost always confident. That's a given if they're ever going to get anything. Sometimes they're cocky. But they're usually men who enjoy many parts of the outdoors, not just hunting."

"Makes sense so far. What else?"

"They have a certain way they like to do things when they hunt. They have established patterns."

She frowned a little and he could tell he'd lost her. "Let me try again. What I mean is that they tend to wear the same clothes. They'll have a favorite jacket, often they're sentimental about a particular gun and prefer to hunt with it."

"They're creatures of habit." McKenna nodded as she took notes.

"Any ideas whether or not the dead men fit that profile?"

She shook her head. "I wish I knew more about them." Her eyes narrowed a little as she focused on a distant spot on the wall. "I feel like there's something in my mind, something about what you just said…"

"It'll come to you."

"Yeah. It will. It has to, because I'm going to solve this case."

In spite of the confident words, Will heard the waver in her tone, wished he could do something to bolster her, help her not doubt herself. But did *he* have full confidence that she could figure this out? He honestly didn't know.

Instead, he reached for her hand, gave it a quick squeeze. "I've got to head to work. You be careful."

She promised she would. And Will prayed she was telling the truth.

SIX

McKenna pored over paperwork in the office at Truman Hunting Expeditions for hours the following day, her attention taken away from her task periodically by Will smiling at her and Rick glaring at her.

The contrast made it difficult to focus.

At just after five, she gave up. She wasn't sure what she was looking for, but she knew she hadn't found it. There was nothing interesting—no names she recognized, no signs of illegal activity.

"Are you done here?" Rick asked her, seeing her standing from her spot at the desk.

"I think I am." She looked around one last time, trying to ignore his tone as she scrutinized the area to make sure there was nothing she'd missed. But everything was as it should have been. Her investigations into the two biggest guide companies in the area had yielded zero results. Frustrated didn't begin to describe the way she was starting to feel. Which was why she paused at the door, turned back to face Rick. "You haven't heard of a guy named Seth Davison, have you?"

Rick shook his head. "I don't think I know him. Why?"

"No reason." She paused. "Actually, there is a reason.

He's dead. And the last thing anyone knew about him, he was up here on a hunting trip."

"You checked my books. I didn't take him."

She had looked specifically for Seth's name, along with the other two. Knew they weren't there. She'd been hoping Rick might give something away if she caught him off guard, but he was either an excellent liar or he had nothing to hide. "All right."

"Maybe he went with another guide service."

She'd checked them all. As far as any of them or their records were concerned, the three men didn't exist.

"No one's heard of him. Thank you for your cooperation," she forced herself to say. Will's boss may not have been polite, but he had been cooperative. And since he was also apparently innocent of any wrongdoing, she needed to make sure to stay on good terms with him, since, given the job, it was inevitable that they would cross paths again.

He seemed to relax. "You're welcome."

"I'm going to head out," Will let Rick know as he gathered his things and followed her.

"See you."

Once they were in the parking lot, McKenna let out a deep breath. "That's not how I expected things to go."

"What do you mean?"

She shook her head. "Let's wait until we're in private. I shouldn't have said anything yet."

They climbed into her car and she drove them to her and Anna's house. Anna wasn't home yet—she must be working late.

"So are you going to tell me what you meant back there in the parking lot?" Will asked once they'd settled in on the living room couch. She'd seated herself next to the arm, leaving plenty of space beside her, but he'd taken the other end of the couch. McKenna wished they were closer. She was pretty sure that after a few minutes of sitting with Will with his arms around her, she'd be able to relax and the headache she was getting from this case would disappear.

She tried to shake the image from her head. As though that scenario would ever happen. He wasn't interested in her in that way. Never had been. Which was why she wouldn't allow herself to get interested in him, either. She wouldn't even let herself ask for comfort—not when she was sure it would only add to his certainty that she was some fragile creature unsuited to handle the stresses of her job.

"I just thought once I found out that the men on the tundra and the one at the beach were hunters… I was probably grasping at straws. Outsiders come here to hunt. Since all three men were nonlocals, it stands to reason that they were hunters. But that might have nothing to do with their deaths at all."

"Hey, don't beat yourself up. It could have and you checked it out."

She shrugged. "I was just so sure I'd found the connection."

"You don't feel like you missed anything, though, do you?"

"No." McKenna didn't hesitate. "I checked everything I could. Your boss may not be the most charming person in the world, but his records check out. I'd say his business is completely legit."

"So where do you focus your attention now?"

"I want to follow up on George, that guy I met last night."

"I doubt you'll find much information about him. He's one of those guys everyone knows but no one knows much about."

"I'm up for the challenge."

"You suspect him because of his opposition to wild-life troopers?"

"Not just that. Last night he seemed downright hostile toward the guy who was dead. Essentially said he'd gotten what was coming to him." Chills ran up and down her spine as she said the words. "If those aren't the words of a potential killer…"

"He could be all talk, though. Guys like him often are."

She thought of the man's smirk, of the depth of hopelessness in his eyes. "And he might not be."

"You're taking a serious risk looking into him any further, McKenna. If he *is* the killer, then he's the same man who broke into your house, who tried to kill us."

"It's my job, Will." How many times did they have to go over this? McKenna couldn't deny the anxious knot in her stomach at the idea of talking to a possible murderer. But it was something she *had* to do.

Will stared at her. She stared back. Unflinching.

Will broke first. "Be careful."

"Always."

"Seriously, Will. I'll be fine," McKenna had said with a smile as she'd said goodbye to him last night. His gut was sick at the thought of her investigating by herself. He wished he could go with her, but the group scheduled for today had been on the calendar for months. He couldn't cancel it. This group was made up of a couple of pastors from Anchorage and some men from their church and since he'd been their guide in years past, they'd asked for him specifically. And if it weren't for his worry over McKenna, he'd be looking forward to it.

Will tossed his duffel bag into his truck and started toward the Truman Hunting Expeditions office. As he pulled up, he surveyed the outside. It was a pretty nice building, well kept anyway. It was essentially a portable structure, about the size of a single-wide trailer. Rick had done a good job maintaining it and keeping up with things like repainting.

Will shut off his truck and let himself into the office. It didn't seem like Rick or Matt were there yet. His clients weren't supposed to arrive for another couple of hours—he couldn't remember the exact time, but knew it was mid-morning—which gave him plenty of time to get things set up for them.

As he walked past Rick's desk, the calendar caught his eye. Thinking Rick might have written down the exact time his clients were arriving, he looked at today's date.

Yep, there they were. Nine-thirty. He'd be ready in plenty of time.

Will started to walk away, but turned back to the calendar. Many of the days in the past few weeks were blank, or only showed hunts he and Matt had led. Not Rick. But Rick had been out of the office, presumably working, several times.

Will frowned and shook his head, knowing his boss's schedule was none of his business. Guilt for looking at the calendar in the first place troubled him, but his intent hadn't been to be nosy. He'd just needed to confirm the time for his trip today.

Still, something about the calendar bothered him as he completed his morning routine and readied the plane for the flight he and his clients would be taking. Maybe Rick had had business meetings on those days he'd been out of the office—with the bank, perhaps, to talk about the financial issues he seemed to be having. But wouldn't those appointments be on the calendar, too? Was Rick leaving the office on those days for something completely unrelated to work? As far as Will knew, Rick and his wife had a decent marriage. But maybe something weird was going on with his boss's personal life that was making him sneak around.

Worst-case scenario, as far as he could guess, was that maybe Rick was taking people hunting off the books. He'd heard of guys doing it before—taking friends for a hunt and accepting the "gift" of money they were given for doing so. That way the money wasn't taxable, a big deal in a business like guided hunting, where one trip could pay upward of ten thousand dollars.

He pushed that suspicion away. Just because Rick was a private guy and didn't run the business the way Will would didn't mean he'd break the law. Besides, McKenna had looked through the important files and paperwork yesterday and hadn't discovered anything out of the ordinary. All the incidents with McKenna's case had made him suspicious of everyone.

Will finished his preflight checklist and sent up a brief prayer, as he always did, that God would protect those on his airplane today and give them success and safety on their hunt.

When his clients showed up, Will had a smile on his face and was more ready than he'd been in a long time to take people out on the tundra to enjoy the sport he loved.

Will's tortured expression from last night haunted McKenna all the way to work. The way he'd begged her, a strange vulnerability in his eyes, not to investigate today without him there, had tugged at her heart. Was it possible his protectiveness wasn't because he thought she was incompetent but just because he didn't want her to get hurt—maybe even because he cared for her? McKenna was afraid to hope that might be the case. So she'd refused his offer, had insisted she'd be fine. But last night had been full of torturous nightmares that reminded her that someone out there wanted her dead, and perhaps it would be wise of her to heed Will's request to wait for his help.

So today she was putting the murder case out of her mind. At least until she got her rounds made checking harvest tickets and hunting licenses to make sure everyone was hunting according to the rules.

This part of the job was something she was relatively familiar with, though she hadn't done it as much when she'd been stationed in Anchorage. There were areas close to the city that were used for hunting, but up here it was a huge part of people's lives.

McKenna had been reviewing all the data she could find in her little office about past cases at this trooper post. It looked as if hunting violations, the issue she was dealing with today, usually happened for the same reasons. Either the person was ignorant—which seemed to be the rarest cause for a violation—or they were deliberately breaking the law, either because they wanted to harvest more than the legal limit or because they'd been too lazy to go through the proper channels.

And then there was the last reason, which was the most difficult for her to deal with. Sometimes native Alaskans would hunt without proper licenses and with no regard to set seasons because their ancestors had done so and they felt it was still their right.

Her mind flashed back to her conversation, or lack thereof, with George the night before on the beach. He had made no secret that he tended toward that view. She knew better than to assume he hunted illegally just because of the beliefs he held about it, but it wouldn't surprise her. She wondered how many others felt the way he did.

McKenna checked her map one last time before folding it up and putting it in the backpack she'd be bringing with her. Today she was taking the ATV out and patrolling the wilderness around Barrow, checking hunters' documents as she came upon them. She was hoping doing so would help her establish herself in the area. It was also something Captain Wilkins had reminded her she needed to do last time they'd talked. Today seemed as good a day as any to do it. She didn't relish the idea of being on the tundra alone, but this was her job. And since it wasn't tied to the investigation, she should be at no more risk than usual. Some of the areas she needed to patrol would've been easier to access by plane, but since Will was working and she certainly wasn't calling Chris, this would have to do.

McKenna shivered even though Chris was nowhere near her, strapped the backpack over the jacket she'd already put on and went outside to finish loading the last of the supplies she'd need for the day. She was almost ready to leave, when the phone in her office rang.

She took the front steps two at a time and snatched the phone up on the sixth ring. "Trooper Clark."

"Don't you sound professional," a male voice teased.

"Luke? Why are you calling here?"

"Because it's where you work. That, and I figured if I called your cell you might ignore me. You can't very well ignore a work call."

He knew her too well. On both counts.

"So, what's up?" she asked, trying to keep her voice light. Was it too much to hope Luke had forgotten about her house being broken into?

"I wanted to see how you are." His voice had deepened into what she recognized as his serious, Protective Older Brother tone. "This case sounds like it has the potential to be dangerous, so I wanted to check on you."

"I'm doing fine. You do stuff like this all the time, Luke."

"Yeah, but you're my little sister. It's my job to look out for you. And Will's, since I asked him to."

Any ideas from the night before that Will might be doing this because of...*feelings* for her evaporated from her mind as the truth settled on her with the grace of an anvil. He was watching out for her because of her relationship with her brother and because Luke, and maybe Will, too, didn't believe she could handle the case on her own.

But she could. She'd just have to show them somehow. "I'm fine," she insisted to Luke, determined not to let him hear how much his words bothered her.

"Just be careful, okay?"

"As much as I can be," McKenna said, her resolve growing. "But I do have to do my job."

"I know. Love you," he added as they prepared to hang up.

Her heart softened a little. He might be overprotective, might be annoyingly competent at his own job sometimes, which made her feel as if she could never measure up, but he was her brother. "Love you, too."

Ten minutes later, she was on a road out of town, headed into the remoteness of the tundra.

Sometimes the sheer vastness of this land overwhelmed her. It was beautiful, especially now, in the last few weeks of summer before winter came—there was no fall this far north. The shades of green were vibrant against a sapphire sky, and the bright pink of blooming fireweed provided more contrast to the scene. It was beautiful. So beautiful it was hard to believe that the land could be so deadly. The contradiction was difficult to wrap her mind around.

Then again, McKenna supposed most things in life were like that—the most dangerous offered the most reward. Will's face flashed into her mind. Oh, yes, giving in to the desire to pursue a relationship with him would be dangerous for sure. There was their history to contend with—their newly re-formed friendship would end if things didn't work out. Besides that, there was the danger of how much she knew she could feel for Will if she let herself. She knew deep in her heart that if she ever allowed herself to fall in love with Will, it would be all at once, with nothing gradual about it, and he'd have her whole heart in his hands. For someone who liked to plan out her life in meticulous detail, that was a dangerous scenario.

She should know. She'd come close once, and look how that had turned out.

Besides, Will didn't see her that way. Shouldn't she have gotten that into her head by now?

McKenna pushed Will from her mind, knowing she had to give all her attention to her job today. As previous days had proven, she needed all her senses on alert, or the results could be disastrous.

SEVEN

McKenna's watch showed it was almost six by the time she pulled the ATV back into Barrow. She'd meant to wrap up a little closer to five, especially since she'd started working well before seven that morning. But she'd been happy with the progress she was making getting to know the area, and hadn't wanted to quit.

She'd half expected to run into Will sometime during the day. Not that she needed to check *his* paperwork. Truman Hunting Expeditions, according to the records her predecessor had left and her own investigations the previous day, was meticulous about having its ducks in a row. She was confident that Will's group would have had their paperwork in order.

Thankfully, everyone she'd come upon that day had been hunting legally. McKenna thought it made her first day doing that task easier since she hadn't needed to arrest or fine anyone.

Now she just had to wrap a few things up and she'd be ready to go home with her notes on the murder case and see what progress she could make.

Her stomach growled, angrily protesting the fact that she'd forgotten to pack a lunch. Maybe she'd see about food first and then work on the case.

She parked the ATV and made her way inside the building. The cool late-afternoon air crept straight through her jacket. Goose bumps rose on the back of her neck and she tried to shrug them away as she fumbled with her key and unlocked the door to the small building.

Uneasiness washed over her. Was she just cold? Or did that uncomfortable feeling come from the awareness of being watched?

She'd felt relatively safe all day. Nothing out of the ordinary had happened. She'd been fine. It had been relaxing, even. Now, in town, she felt on edge again. It didn't make sense.

McKenna finished what she needed to do and walked to a window, moving one blind slightly to peer out and look for anything out of the ordinary.

Everything looked as it should.

She was being paranoid. McKenna glanced down at her watch. It was well after six now and her stomach was no longer just protesting—it was demanding food. Since she had none in her office, she was going to have to leave.

She flipped the light off, let herself out and locked the door behind her, noting that the moment she stepped outside again she immediately felt aware of something watching her every move.

McKenna walked a little faster, wishing she'd driven that morning. Her house was easily within walking distance, but she hailed the first cab she saw anyway, thankful that they were plentiful, even in a town as small as Barrow. She'd been surprised to see so many when she arrived in town, but their overabundance had certainly come in handy tonight.

"Too cold to walk tonight?" the man asked in a friendly tone as she climbed in. Clearly, he was accustomed to shuttling people short distances because of the weather.

She nodded. "Yeah. Too cold." She said the words absently as she watched through the window to see if any cars made a move to follow them. None of them did. She had to be being paranoid.

She paid the cabbie after he pulled in front of her house and hurried inside as fast as she could, desperately trying to stop thinking of all the terrible scenarios that hovered in her mind as dismal possibilities. She knew it was good for her to be on her guard, but she wasn't used to doing it constantly. McKenna was a wildlife trooper on purpose, not a cop like her brother. She just wasn't made for this nonstop pressure.

"How was your day?" Anna asked as McKenna shut the door and reached down to pet the dogs. Her roommate was curled up on the couch with a mug of what McKenna guessed was hot chocolate. Anna practically lived on the stuff.

McKenna shrugged. "Nothing out of the ordinary."

"Which is normally good. But I guess not right now, with the case you're working."

"I need a new lead. Desperately."

"I'll keep my eyes open," Anna offered.

McKenna shook her head. "No, I don't want you to risk it."

"Oh, I won't do any investigating myself—but if something catches my eye, I'll let you know. Hey, by the way, did I tell you my parents sent me a stack of books in the mail today?"

"Ooooh."

"I'm going to go take a bath and read, I think," Anna finally proclaimed in a determined voice. "I need a good, funny book to take my mind off of all I've heard from you and Will about this case lately." She turned as she left the room, a sly smile edging across her face. "Although, speaking of romance…" She winked and then left before McKenna could protest.

Romance? No. She might have feelings for him, but he just saw her as a friend. Worse, he saw her as Luke's little sister.

Her phone made its text message noise. It was Will. As if he'd read her mind and realized she was thinking of him.

She opened the message.

Missed you today. Any chance I could convince you to run away with me tomorrow? To hang out and go four-wheeling or something?

McKenna would never admit to anyone the butterflies she'd gotten when she'd read that second sentence, before Will clarified. It was ridiculous, really. She should know he wouldn't ever mean anything like that in relation to her.

Then again, he did want to spend time with her. Time that clearly wouldn't be focused on work. Wasn't that a little like a date?

McKenna shook her head, hoping to shake some sense into her obviously overtired brain. This was Will.

She texted Will back.

Can't tomorrow. I need to see if I can turn up any leads on this case.

His reply came after only seconds. That's what I meant—I thought we could go four-wheeling and keep our eyes open for anything that might relate to your case.

Of course that's what he'd meant. Heat flooded her cheeks. When he put it that way, it was a pretty good idea. She'd tapped out most of the resources she could find in town. If she was going to learn anything new, she'd have to expand her boundaries. Until something else happened, she was stuck anyway. Maybe the chance to take a break from being in the office would help her think. Better yet, maybe they would actually run into someone who had seen suspicious activity on the day the hunters were killed.

Yeah, of course. Sure, let's do it.

She tossed the phone down and went to tell Anna her plans through the closed bathroom door. Anna told her to have fun, making some more cracks about hers and Will's so-called "relationship." McKenna laughed and was still laughing as she walked down the hallway to her own room. She wouldn't have thought she'd like having a roommate, but Anna was fun. She was becoming a good friend faster than McKenna would have thought possible, so that was one positive that had come from all of this. She should focus on that.

"Your brother and I used to do this a lot—borrow our parents' four-wheelers and ride all over," Will commented as he readied the four-wheelers for their trip.

"I remember." McKenna raised her eyebrows. "I always wanted to go and you'd never let me."

"No, *Luke* would never let you." Whether it was because he didn't want his little sister tagging along, or because he'd suspected his best friend had a thing for his little sister, Will didn't know. He'd never asked. His feelings for McKenna were something he'd never liked to think about.

They rode in silence through town until Will pulled off the road to park his truck at the edge of Barrow, the farthest they could drive before switching to the four-wheelers.

McKenna laid a hand on his arm. Just that soft touch probably made his heart skip at least half a beat.

"Can I ask you a question?" Her voice was quiet. Not demanding. Not teasing.

Which made him wonder how serious a question this was going to be. Not that it mattered—he'd always been able to talk to her about anything. He shifted in his seat. "Sure. What is it?"

She studied his face for a minute. "Why are you up here? I mean, I know you wanted to get out of Seward, see more of Alaska. And that you were never big on cities."

"Unlike you."

She shrugged. "Yeah, unlike me…"

Her voice trailed off, almost as if she was asking herself the same question Will had asked himself a hundred times. If they'd been more similar, if their dreams about their adult lives had been more in line, would they have tried out the idea of a relationship?

No, they were too different in other ways. And she was still his best friend's sister.

"Anyway. What brings me up here? That's what you're wondering?"

She smiled, almost shyly. "Yeah."

"After Rachael died…" He stumbled over her name, feeling odd for some reason about mentioning his wife by name to McKenna. "I knew I wanted to get even farther from the city. I was living in Palmer at the time, so it wasn't too big of a town, but I wanted smaller."

"Why not just go back to Seward?"

He shrugged. "Partly like you said before. There was more of Alaska I wanted to see." That and facing his hometown, the familiar life he'd always known with the weight of losing his wife pressing against him from every angle, had seemed like more than he'd be able to bear.

"So you ended up here." She raised her eyebrows. "In the bush. With a business degree."

He laughed, thankful for the lighter note the conversation had struck. "It's not as crazy as it sounds. I'm planning to use that degree here one day, you know."

"Working at Truman Hunting Expeditions?"

The thought of work made his throat tight. The job he'd once loved became more and more stressful every day, with the new type of clients who kept coming in. "No. That's not something I want to do for much longer."

"What do you want to do?" Her voice was sweet and curious. As if she genuinely cared.

Part of him wanted her to care.

"I want to have my own business." Will looked at her, searched her eyes for any sign that she thought he was crazy, that this dream of his was too big. He didn't see any doubt in her expression. Only an excitement that mirrored his own.

"Will!" she exclaimed. "You'd be great at that! Hunting has always been a passion of yours, I know, and you do it so well and so responsibly. And that would put that business degree to good use."

A degree she'd helped him decide on during one of their long conversations years ago. He'd been so uncertain about his future, but she'd always been able to see his strengths and encourage him to pursue them. "Thanks. I'm not sure when I'll do it, but it's an idea anyway."

"I think it's a great one."

The way she smiled at him, as if he was some kind of dream come true, took him off guard. He wanted to do something to get that look off her face. He was nobody's dream come true. Even if McKenna…intrigued him and always had, he wasn't starting out fresh the way she was in life. He couldn't possibly take the risks another relationship would require. She'd be better off thinking of him as she always had. As a friend.

Because it was all he could ever be to her.

"Come on." He nodded toward the waiting tundra as he opened the door of his truck. "Help me get these unloaded. We have a full day of four-wheeling ahead."

"So, about earlier," McKenna began as she loaded her gun into one of the cargo bags on the four-wheeler.

"What about it?"

McKenna watched him, studied his eyes as he watched her. She felt her cheeks flush and silently called herself ridiculous. There was nothing life changing in the question she was about to ask. She was just curious. That was all.

"You said *Luke* would never let me tag along."

Silence stretched between them until Will said, "Yeah."

"Would you have let me come?"

He held her gaze, and her heart fluttered as emotions she was sure she was making up danced in the depths of Will's eyes. "I might have."

The boldness that seemed to have suddenly come over her vanished just as quickly. "Well…" McKenna couldn't contain the nervous laughter. "We'll have to do some serious riding today, then. Make up for lost time."

He watched her for a minute and then finally nodded. "Yeah. That sounds good." He turned away to ready his four-wheeler, and McKenna was left almost breathless. *What* sounded good? Serious riding, or making up for lost time?

"There's a river up here." Will motioned. "It's not too far." He grinned. "I'll race you to it, if you think you can keep up."

"You're on." She took the challenge and they were off.

They rode for hours, occasionally stopping to take a drink from their water bottles or eat a quick snack before hitting the trail again. McKenna kept her eyes open for any signs of other people whom she could potentially interview. People who loved the land had special insights to offer—if she could find someone out here, maybe they'd have information that could help her in her investigation. But so far it was just her and Will. She signaled to him that she was stopping for a bathroom break and he waved his acknowledgment as he continued up the trail.

Pulling over, a glance down at her clothes had confirmed McKenna's suspicions that she was covered in dust and must look like a mess, but she didn't care.

When she was ready to go again, McKenna gunned the engine, eager to get back to Will. Its roar filled her ears and the cool wind whipped her face. She knew her cheeks would be red and her lips would be chapped by the time this day was done, but it would be worth it.

She pressed the gas harder, flying over the trail. Uneasiness crawled up her spine and neck and she sent a glance over her shoulder.

Not fifty feet behind her was another ATV. And it wasn't Will's; he was up ahead of her. Whoever was driving this one was hunched over, dressed in all black and wearing a mask.

She sped up a little, hoping it was just coincidence, that maybe a perfectly nice man had decided to go for a ride on the same trail they had, dressed in all black. Nothing nefarious. Just a coincidence.

He sped up, too. So much for that.

McKenna glanced around her, looking for a place she could cut off of the main trail and lose him in the vastness of the tundra. For once she wished she'd been living here longer—so she'd know all the shortcuts and places to hide.

As it was, she could veer off the trail, but she was so unfamiliar with the territory that it might end up being a bad move. She could be lost forever out here.

No, it was better to stick to the route she knew. Will shouldn't be too far ahead. If only she could reach him before the mystery man reached her.

The world slowed as the ATV slammed into her from behind and McKenna fought two warring impulses—hang on with all her might, or let go so she wasn't crushed if another attack came.

The question was answered for her as he hit her a second time. As metal crunched, she was thrown from the seat of the machine. She landed on the cold ground with a hard thud. She scrambled to stand immediately and ran in the direction where she knew Will was waiting, a scream building in her throat.

Heavy footfalls behind her left no doubt that the stranger was pursuing her. The crash must have knocked him off his four-wheeler, too. McKenna pushed herself as hard as she could, feeling her muscles burning but ignoring their protests.

Her shoulder took the force of the impact as he tackled her and she found herself falling to the ground.

"Will! Help!" She yelled the words as loud as she could but the wind snatched them away. She had no idea if she'd been loud enough for him to hear.

McKenna's attacker clapped a heavy, gloved hand over her mouth with one hand, and with the other reached to his side.

The menacing black handgun he pulled out made her heart skip. As long as they were fighting hand to hand, she stood a chance. Not much of one, but a chance anyway. She was unarmed, though, with her own weapon back with the four-wheeler, and could do nothing against a gun.

Desperation propelling her motions, she flailed and knocked the gun from his hand. He watched it fly through the air and land ten feet away or so. She hoped he'd go after it and give her a chance to escape.

Instead, he pulled something from his pocket—a long, dangerous-looking knife with some kind of white carved handle and a silver blade that glittered menacingly in the sunlight.

As he raised his arm, McKenna kicked with all her might, but nothing she did allowed her to overpower him. "Will!" she yelled one last time, knowing if the knife came down and found its target, it wouldn't matter how fast he got there, it would be too late.

The sun glinted and flickered off the knife and her attacker gave a hint of a smile at the despair that must be showing on her face.

A shiver ran through her as she took a deep breath, realizing this was probably the end.

As the man's arm tensed and he began to bring the knife down, a blur behind him made McKenna's eyes widen. Will knocked the man sideways in a tackle and the two of them grappled on the ground, the attacker still wielding the knife and Will, as far as she could tell, unarmed.

She stood and moved away from the fight, wanting to help but knowing from experience that getting in the middle of the fight was as likely to cause problems as do any good. With the knife, the attacker had the stronger position, and she wouldn't risk distracting Will at the wrong moment. She considered running back to the four-wheeler for her gun, but knew it would be useless to try to aim while the men were tangled up fighting. Hitting Will was too big of a risk.

After another minute of struggling, Will managed to wrench the knife from the man's hand. Seeing he'd lost his advantage, the attacker freed himself from Will's grasp and ran to reholster his gun. Stunned, McKenna stared for a second, then pulled herself off the ground and chased him as fast as she could.

She'd almost caught him when he jumped back on his four-wheeler and gunned it. McKenna ran to hers, climbed on and pushed the starter button. Nothing happened. She tried again, mashing the throttle to rev the engine.

The smell of gasoline and the refusal of the machine to start told her she'd flooded the engine.

She'd have to wait to try again.

McKenna shut the machine off, climbed down and kicked one of the tires. So close. Yet he still got away.

EIGHT

Will gripped the knife in his hands, taking deep breaths as he fought to regain control over the surging waves of what he guessed might be adrenaline. He sat up and stared at the shaking of his hands. The knife fell from his grasp, onto the grass.

He looked up at McKenna, half wondering if he'd dreamed the entire scene. The haunted look in her widened eyes told him he hadn't. It had been all too real. As if the knife he'd been holding hadn't been enough proof.

"Are you okay?" He finally forced the words out as he stood, scanning her for injuries. He saw none, but still needed the reassurance.

"I d-don't know," she stuttered. "I mean, yes. I think."

She sounded so vulnerable, so shaken, he didn't know what else he could do but pull her into his arms.

He'd expected her to resist, to protest somehow, but instead she turned her face into his chest and began to cry.

Will kept a careful watch on their surroundings as he held her. He was relatively certain the threat was over for now, but it never hurt to be careful. Still, he was grateful McKenna was taking a break. She needed someone to help her carry this load—he could see how much it was weighing on her. And he wanted to be that person.

He tightened his arms around her and bent to her ear. "It's really going to be okay. Soon."

Will thought he heard her sniff.

Eventually, she pulled away. Will's arms felt empty without her in them. He could face down just about anything the Alaskan wilderness had to offer and not flinch. But the way he was starting to feel about McKenna scared him. If anyone else described these feelings to him, he'd say they were in love. No hesitation. But with him and McKenna…it had to be something else. Just a close-friendship kind of feeling? Crazy emotions from the danger and stress?

Some part of him knew otherwise, knew better, but he wasn't ready to go there yet. He shoved the thoughts away, knowing distraction could get them both killed. Or worse, get her killed and leave him dealing with the guilt at not having kept her safe.

He already knew all too well how that felt.

"What now?" he asked.

"I'll need that knife." McKenna dug through her backpack until she came up with a brown paper bag. "For evidence. I'll send it to the crime lab in Anchorage for processing. One of the guys working forensics there is one of the best in the nation, Luke says. If there's something to find, he'll find it."

"You haven't heard back on the evidence from the first crime scene yet, have you?"

She shook her head. "It's not like you see on TV. That kind of information takes a few weeks to get, usually. I should hear soon, though."

"Not soon enough to suit me."

McKenna shrugged. "Me neither, but that's how it is."

"Ready to head back?" he asked her after she'd snapped some pictures of the area, treating it as a crime scene.

"I guess so."

"We've got a long ride." He caught her gaze and held it. "Are you okay to drive or should you ride with me? We could come back for your four-wheeler later."

"I'll be okay." She smiled a little and hesitated over the next words. "But it's sweet of you to ask."

McKenna seemed surprised at his concern, had seemed even more surprised by his embrace earlier. Did she really not have a clue to the depth of the feelings he had for her—that he'd *always* had for her, even before he left their little town for Anchorage all those years ago?

Those feelings were part of the reason he'd left. She'd always been off-limits, and too many times on the rocky beach at Resurrection Bay, he'd almost kissed her and crossed the invisible line they'd drawn between friends and something more. It wasn't just his friendship with Luke that had stopped him, although that had been a big part of it. It had been the knowledge that if they started to date and it didn't work out, he would lose McKenna's friendship. He hadn't had many good things in his childhood, and he wasn't going to risk one of the relationships that meant the most to him for a silly teenage crush.

Maybe the lengths he'd been willing to go to in order to make sure that didn't happen should have given him a clue that he'd cared about her more than he realized, even then. But it hadn't.

"I really did have fun today," McKenna insisted again as they drove down the road in his truck, the trailer pulling the four-wheelers behind them.

Will grimaced. "You mean before someone chased you down and tried to kill you?"

"Tried. I'm okay, Will. Would you quit worrying?"

He didn't know how to tell her that the nagging, churning feeling in his gut when it came to her safety was something that had been there for quite a few years—he was pretty convinced it wasn't leaving anytime soon.

If he could turn off the protective instincts, he would. No, that wasn't right. She was still a friend, and he wanted to do everything in his power to keep her safe. But he could feel his heart wavering between the kind of caring one gives to a friend's safety and something more and he wished there was a way to shut down those feelings.

Hadn't he learned his lesson about relationships with daring women? He'd loved every minute he'd had with Rachael, loved her with all the love he had to give. But she'd had adventures to chase and those adventures had eventually taken her from him.

McKenna was even more of a spitfire than Rachael had ever been. More independent. And in the week since she'd been back in his life, she'd managed to get herself in more trouble than he'd thought one woman could get in.

How did she report to a new job and find someone trying to kill her almost from day one?

Will bristled. "McKenna, do you ever wonder if it's not just coincidence that has you in someone's sights? Like, maybe you're an intentional target—not just the person who happened to find the bodies."

"Is that your way of saying you're going to ignore the request not to worry?"

"Yeah. For the moment I am. Now, focus on my theory. What do you think?"

She paused, seeming to consider it. "I can see it. It's not too outrageous. But why? I'm just your average run-of-the-mill wildlife trooper." She shrugged. "Nothing special."

He'd argue with her there, awareness of her specialness seemed to be distracting him from just about everything these days. "What about Luke? Isn't he working some high-profile case?"

That seemed to get her attention. "You're thinking this is tied to the Davis case?"

"Yeah. He mentioned it was really important. Living up here I haven't heard details. Remind me what's going on with it."

"There's not much to tell, unfortunately. They haven't been able to get any solid leads. Several months ago Maggie Davis disappeared from the grocery store she worked at, never to be heard from again."

"Maybe Luke's getting close to something. Maybe the guy behind it is trying to distract Luke by going after his family. It's been done before."

She wrinkled her nose. "Yeah, it has. It's pretty cliché, actually. I doubt it."

"I'm not ready to dismiss any valid theories," he insisted as they bumped over the gravel road that was taking them closer to Barrow by the minute.

McKenna pulled out her cell phone. "Fine. I'll text Luke and see if he's gotten any new leads lately. But I'm not going to tell him about this ridiculous theory because he worries worse than you do."

Her thumbs flew over the screen of the phone and then she set it down, giving him a look. "Are you happy?"

"Happier." He was pretty sure he couldn't be completely happy until this danger was behind them. "Do you have any theories, since you don't seem to buy into mine?" Will asked, changing the subject but keeping it focused on the case because he was afraid of where their conversation would go if they didn't stick to work. The times from earlier in the day when they'd almost brought up their past and all the might-have-beens that needed to stay there had been too numerous for comfort. This was a safer subject.

McKenna considered his question, her face edged into a frown as she did so. "I have a few, yes."

Subject changed. Will felt his shoulders relax. "Like what?"

"Well…" she began. "Let's go back to square one."

"Which is?"

"The initial murders. Which, like you've pointed out, I discovered because of the tip that someone might be poaching there. Because of that—the initial incident—I have a few main suspects." She looked at him warily. "I'm not 100 percent sure you're going to be happy with them."

What did she mean by that? Surely she didn't suspect him; they went too far back for that. Will shrugged. "They're your suspects."

"Okay." She paused again. "You're sure you want to hear?"

"Yeah, I'm sure."

"The first one is that George guy."

"And why do you suspect him?"

McKenna twisted uncomfortably. "It was the way he said things that night on the beach. Like he knew more than he was saying. And the way he smirked… He sounded like he was glad the other man had died. And he brought up hunting regulations."

"Which doesn't make someone a criminal."

She glared at him. Will threw up his hands in mock surrender. "Just trying to play the other side here, make you think through things."

"I think he's involved. Somehow," she said. Will didn't know George well enough to comment on his character. And what she said did make sense, he just wanted to make sure she had solid proof before she went around accusing people.

Then again, *she* was the one who was supposed to be investigating, wasn't she? "Okay, who else?"

A shadow darkened her expression. "Chris. The pilot the troopers had assigned to me."

"I think I know who you're talking about. I don't know him, but I've seen him around town. Is he an actual trooper?"

She shook her head. "No, but he's on the payroll. He knows people in the department. I hate to suspect him because of that, but he didn't seem surprised when we stumbled upon those bodies. It was like he kept watching me to see my reaction, but he never had one himself."

That was odd.

"The way he watched me… I don't have a good feeling in my gut about him."

"That also sounds logical. But if he was behind the murders, why didn't he kill you right there, then?"

McKenna shrugged. "I haven't figured that part out yet. This case seems to have several layers. And the last person I'm really looking at right now…" She drew a deep breath. "He has a connection to your hunting company. It would be logical for an actual hunting service to be involved in this, even though yours has a good reputation."

Will bristled. "I might not always like the kind of clients he takes on, but Rick is too smart, too much of a straight-lines kind of guy to get involved in something so drastically illegal."

McKenna's face was blank and impassive. "I wasn't talking about Rick. I was talking about Matt."

"Matt?" The question exploded out of him even as he felt his face heat and his blood pressure begin to rise. "You're putting one of my best friends up there on your suspect list to be investigated? Is this list official in any way? Are other people going to come after him? Because you could end up ruining his life."

"Didn't you tell me he had a criminal past?"

Will flexed his grip on the steering wheel, squeezing tight and then letting go to help release the pressure he felt building up inside of him. "I told you that to help you understand where he and his wife were coming from, why they'd understand what you're going through."

"Well, he has the opportunity to have committed such a crime, with all that time he spends alone on the tundra with various people."

"So do I," Will countered, defending his friend. "So does my boss, for that matter."

"But I checked out the official business records and those seem to indicate Rick's clean. Besides, neither of you has a criminal record." Her face had hardened now; her gaze was all business. "That stands against Matt."

"But you don't have any evidence?"

"Nothing solid—against him or anyone else. But we have opportunity, and money is always a good motivator. Didn't you say things have been rough for them lately?"

"Things have been rough for everyone. What makes you think he'd do something illegal?"

She shrugged. "He has before. And now he has a wife to take care of. He feels responsible for providing and business is tough. People have broken the law for less."

Will jerked the truck over to the side of the road, suddenly unable to focus on driving. He turned to McKenna. "You know what? I know some of that looks bad. But Matt is not your guy. I know him, and if you trust me at all, you'll cross him off that list and look somewhere else."

His chest tightened when she didn't immediately nod. He watched as she stared out the window, off into the distance somewhere. Finally she turned to him, slowly, and spoke. "I'm sorry you're taking this so hard. I didn't say I wanted to suspect him. But several things point to him as a possible suspect. And until I have a solid reason not to, he's staying on that list."

She held his gaze, not flinching. Will tried not to take it personally. Matt probably wouldn't. But for some reason, the combination of her suspecting a good friend of his, and not trusting his word that she didn't need to, rankled him. He put the truck back in drive and continued down the road. The crunch of gravel beneath the tires was the only sound for several miles.

The chirp of a text message notification on McKenna's phone broke the silence. She glanced down at it and read the message. He glanced over at her.

"It's from Luke." McKenna's face had been drained of all its color. "He says they're getting close to finding this guy." She swallowed hard. "And he said that one of the other officers on the Davis case has had family members get threatening notes. And just last night someone made an attempt on one of their lives." She gulped. "He says to be careful. That the guy could come after me next."

McKenna watched expressions chase across Will's face and wondered briefly if he knew how much of his thoughts she could see clearly in his bright blue eyes.

He was mad. And she got that. She'd be mad, too, in his shoes, but she had to investigate everyone who seemed like a reasonable suspect. So far, Matt's background seemed more than a little suspicious. Unfortunately.

But she'd watched the anger on Will's face morph into fear due to the message Luke had sent, and then into concern, presumably for her.

"So I guess your theory might not be as crazy as I

thought," she offered lamely, hoping he'd be able to move past the fact that she'd unintentionally offended him.

"Sounds like it." His voice was gruff. When he didn't add anything else, she turned back to look out the window again. They were approaching her house.

"Thanks for today," she said quietly as she unbuckled her seat belt and eased the passenger-side door open. "For the most part, I enjoyed it. And as for the less enjoyable parts...thank you for protecting me."

She stepped out of the car, hoping Will would say something, anything, to bridge the awkward distance that had sprung up between them.

"I'll unload your four-wheeler for you."

At least he still cared, at least a little, if he was willing to do that. McKenna nodded. "Thanks. Need some help?"

"Nah. Go ahead inside. I'm sure you're tired."

She was, but she had a feeling he was more interested in getting her to leave him alone than in the rest she might need. Will was the kind of guy who'd need time to process if he was going to get over the bomb she'd apparently dropped when she'd mentioned Matt's name. She'd anticipated he'd be upset, but hadn't realized how personally he'd take it.

Of course, she realized as she climbed the steps to the front door, that was how Will was. He was a loyal friend. She knew from watching him grow up that he didn't let that many people too close to him, but once he did, he was invested in that relationship.

She hated that she'd hurt him.

McKenna eased the front door open. It wasn't locked, so Anna must be home. She was careful to reach an arm down and be ready to block one or both of the dogs from escaping. They'd gotten it into their heads lately that they should try to run out every time the door was open.

But neither dog greeted her at the door. McKenna tensed and raised her gun, hoping she didn't scare Anna, but feeling uneasy enough that she felt she should investigate the silent house with it out and ready. She looked back outside to where Will was still working but decided against bothering him. He was already irritated with her, there was no sense in playing damsel-in-distress and drafting him to be her unwilling knight-in-shining-armor yet again.

She dropped her backpack next to the door and left the door open, so that if something was wrong, Will could at least hear her scream for help. Though she was hoping it wouldn't come to that.

Then she heard Mollie whimper from somewhere in the back of the house. McKenna's stomach clenched as she hurried down the hallway to where she'd heard the noise. She prepared herself for the worst, hating the idea that something could have happened to her faithful four-legged friend.

But when she turned the corner into her bedroom, she found that Mollie was physically fine. So was Checkers.

It was Anna, lying on the bloodstained carpet, who wasn't fine.

McKenna was overwhelmed by dizziness at the violence in front of her. She swallowed hard, every feeling she'd had at earlier crime scenes washing over her again, magnified because this wasn't just a victim. It was someone she knew. A friend.

McKenna moved toward her, not wanting to check for a pulse because she feared, judging by the amount of blood, that she wouldn't find one. And if Anna was dead, it was all her fault. She'd brought this danger here. Guilt and desperation to do something to help churned in her stomach as she tried to take deep breaths to keep herself from passing out.

As she reached for Anna's wrist, she took in the evidence she could see. Anna had been shot low on her left shoulder. It looked as if someone had been aiming for her heart and missed. At least, McKenna hoped they'd missed. She didn't know how many inches were between the gunshot wound and the heart, and the best-qualified person to answer that question was bleeding on the floor.

"Hang on, Anna. I'm going to do the best I can." McKenna winced as she reached for Anna's hand, praying it wouldn't be cold. Closing her eyes against the scene, she moved her fingers along her wrist, feeling for a pulse.

It was there. It was weak, but it was there. And that was all that mattered.

"Will!" she yelled as she got to her feet and headed for the door. "Help!"

The dogs, who'd been faithfully keeping watch over Anna, were in a panic now, not sure if they should follow McKenna out or stay.

"You stay," she told them, motioning with her hand so they'd obey. "I'll be right back, Anna," she promised her friend. "I'm going to get help." She pulled her phone out of her pocket, dialing for emergency help as she ran. Gasping for breath between words, she explained the situation to the best of her ability to the dispatcher on the other end, who assured her they'd send paramedics immediately.

"Please let her be okay, God." McKenna whispered the desperate prayer on her way out the front door. Will was just climbing back into his truck, but stopped when he saw her, the puzzled look on his face evidence that he hadn't heard her call for help.

"What's wrong?"

"It's Anna." McKenna felt her hands start to shake, adrenaline starting to fade and give way to shock. "She's been shot."

"Get me some towels."

She hurried to do so, cringing as she grabbed a stack of Anna's fluffy towels from the bathroom and ran back to Will. She knew they might be what saved Anna's life, but somehow ruining the towels seemed sad.

The entire scene was surreal.

Will said nothing for a minute, just applied pressure with the towels, keeping his eyes fixed on Anna's face. He stayed there, seeming to remain calm, until the paramedics arrived and took over the scene.

"Is she going to make it?" McKenna finally found the courage to whisper as some of Anna's coworkers carried her out on a stretcher. The gravity of the situation showed on their faces. McKenna had already known it was bad— the location of the wound and the amount of blood lost had testified to that. But she'd hoped people with medical training would view it as less critical than she feared it was.

Judging by the looks they'd given each other, it was incredibly serious.

Still, she looked to Will, hoping he could give her some kind of reassurance.

He hesitated.

It was all the answer McKenna needed. She sank onto the floor, wrapped her arms around both dogs and cried until she'd soaked their fur with tears.

NINE

The hospital waiting room in Anchorage was exactly the same as it had been last time he'd set foot in it. The day he'd lost his wife.

Will swallowed hard and tried to focus on a point on the dingy tile floor as he blinked back the moisture building in his eyes.

He'd been alone that day. Just as scared as he was now, but worse since it had been someone he deeply loved whose life hung in the balance. While Anna was a dear friend, nothing was the same as losing your wife.

Someone squeezed his hand. He met McKenna's eyes and tried to smile. Today he wasn't alone. And someone else needed him to be the strong one. He tried again to come up with a more reassuring smile. "The doctors here are incredible. And they'll do everything they can for her."

McKenna nodded. "I know. And God is with her."

Hours had passed since they'd discovered Anna. She'd initially been flown to the hospital in Fairbanks, but then transferred to Anchorage when the doctors realized the extensive amount of surgery she'd need.

Will studied McKenna. The tears she'd cried hours before in Barrow had left her eye makeup a little streaked, but as messy as she looked, she seemed more at peace now than she had then.

"When will we know something?" Will turned to ask Matt, who'd come with Lexi as soon as they'd heard.

"The doctor said they'd be out to tell us something as soon as they've finished with the surgery."

Will nodded, looking at Lexi's quiet form, curled up on the seat beside her husband. "Is she okay?" he mouthed, realizing what a stupid question it was as the words left his lips.

Matt's expression said he understood. He looked down at Lexi and shrugged. "They were really close."

"Are," Lexi corrected him. "We *are* close. She isn't… She's not…" She choked back a sob and buried her face in her arms.

But she might be soon. The fact that no one spoke up to reassure Anna's already-grieving sister confirmed that.

No one said anything for a long time.

"I hate hospitals," Will heard himself mutter aloud, breaking the silence.

"Can't say I blame you," McKenna replied.

He wasn't sure he'd meant to say the words aloud. But he was having a hard time keeping himself focused on the present, when memories from the past kept threatening from every corner of the building. "I spent a lot of time here," he said, not sure why he was still talking.

"I'm sure."

Several minutes of silence passed. Will felt McKenna's eyes on his face but didn't turn to meet her gaze. Finally, she spoke. "It's not your fault, you know."

McKenna's eyes were an even deeper green than usual, compassion pooling in their depths. As close as they'd once been, it made sense that she understood, even though no one else ever had. And he wasn't sure if he wanted her to or not.

"What do you mean?" he asked, deciding maybe he'd rather play dumb.

"Rachael's death. I read the article about it in Seward's paper. From the description of where and when she was skiing, it looked like the perfect setup for an avalanche." She paused. "You knew she was going, right?"

She asked it as if she already knew the answer. But he nodded anyway.

"I know you, Will. I know you would have tried to talk her out of it. But she was her own person. And trying to convince her was all you could do. In the end, it was her choice." She said the next words deliberately, slowly, as if to emphasize how strongly she believed them. "It wasn't your fault."

His wife had always been independent, had never really *needed* him. And the one time she did, he hadn't managed to help her, to save her.

He couldn't expect McKenna to get that. "I had a responsibility," he said, his jaw tightening.

"And you did the best you could. You're not God, Will. All you can do is your best."

For once, Will had no desire to talk to McKenna. She hadn't been through what he had. And there was no way she could understand.

"Lexi Dixon?" a man in scrubs asked as he entered the room from behind one of the closed doors.

Lexi sat up. "Yes?"

"Your sister is in very serious condition."

McKenna held her breath.

"But the surgery went well and barring additional complications…I think she's going to be okay."

McKenna's relief was instantly replaced by the fear that whoever had taken a shot at Anna would return to finish the job. As she tried to banish the unpleasant thought from her mind, more questions surfaced.

Why Anna?

Was it possible that whoever was after McKenna would kill someone just for helping her, as Anna had done? That seemed extreme, especially since Anna's biggest contribution had been giving McKenna a place to stay—something that didn't connect her to the case at all. Did logic really say that there was more to Anna's attack? Or was McKenna's desire to avoid adding more guilt to her conscience than she already felt clouding her vision from seeing things as they really were?

"Thank you so much." Lexi's thankful words, muffled by the sounds of her tears, finally registered in McKenna's distracted mind. She looked at her roommate's sister and found that the expression that had been so crushed and hopeless not long ago was now filled with peace and the expectation that everything was going to be okay.

McKenna could only hope that was true. But the more time she spent trying to figure out who wanted her dead and why, the more cynical she became. She wondered if Luke had that problem, too, if it was just a side effect of the job.

"I'm so glad she's okay," she whispered to Will, hoping his earlier mood had passed. McKenna hadn't realized she'd crossed a line and said too much until it was already too late.

He nodded. "Me, too."

McKenna exhaled, thankful he'd let it drop. She slid out of the plastic waiting-room chair and stood. "I'm afraid I have to be leaving."

"It's already dark," Lexi protested. "Don't try to find anyone to fly you up. I'll just worry. You don't want me to worry more than I already am about Anna, do you?"

"I'm not going to Barrow. Not yet. I'll be back here in the morning to check on Anna's progress and then I'll fly up later."

Will stood to follow her. McKenna didn't see any point in telling him not to come with her since she knew he wouldn't listen anyway.

"Where are you going, if you don't mind my asking?" Matt spoke up, gaze darting between Will and McKenna.

"To work on the case," she told him, feeling a little bad she'd ever suspected him of being behind everything. There was no way he'd ever hurt Anna, which meant he couldn't have been responsible for the rest of it, either. "I'm going to do everything I can to make this stop."

"Be careful," Matt warned.

Her roommate was lying in the ICU of a hospital. Blood stained the floor of her bedroom in what was now a crime scene.

McKenna already had all the warning she needed.

She nodded, walking toward the exit door with Will trailing behind.

McKenna stepped out into the parking lot, pulling her light jacket tight around herself. She scanned her surroundings as she walked, hoping exhaustion wouldn't cause her to miss anything she needed to see.

She checked the time on her cell phone and sent a quick text, hating the feeling of needing to ask for help but knowing it had to be done. Up until now, solving this case had been about McKenna, about keeping herself alive and proving her abilities as a trooper. And those goals had been good motivation to do the best she could to solve this case quickly. But now people around her were becoming targets. Her mind couldn't even wrap itself around Will hurt—or worse—because of her. Tears stung her eyes as she thought again of Anna, of finding her bleeding on the carpet, of wondering if she was going to die.

No, the murderer had made the wrong choice when he decided to bring her friends into this. Her best hadn't been good enough to solve this so far, so she'd have to try to do more than her best. If she had to eat, sleep and breathe this case until that man was behind bars, she'd do it.

And going to see Luke was step one on the way to that goal.

"Do you mind sharing the plan, here?" Will asked after he'd followed McKenna around the hospital parking lot for ten minutes while she texted.

He didn't know who she was texting. Or why. But he knew she'd have a plan. McKenna always did. Maybe that's what she was thinking so deeply about now—she'd gone utterly silent, closing him out from whatever thoughts she was having behind those too-serious eyes. More than anything else, that seriousness scared him.

She jumped about a foot in the air.

Then whirled around and glared. "Trying to scare a couple more years off my life? I think I've lost plenty already these past few weeks."

So besides her unusual silence and seriousness, she wasn't paying attention to her surroundings either. In normal circumstances, that was dangerous enough. These circumstances were far from normal and not being aware of her surrounds could get her killed.

The thought chilled him to the core.

"We're going to Luke's," she told him just as a car started toward them. The headlights cutting through the blackness obscured his vision. He was instantly aware of how easy a target they'd be.

"Watch out."

He threw an arm in front of McKenna to stop her as she stepped toward the car. Had she completely abandoned common sense?

"Relax. It's Luke. I texted him and told him where to pick us up."

The car stopped in front of them, and as she'd said, it was Luke in the driver's seat.

"Will! It's been too long, man. You've got to come to the city more often," Luke said as Will and McKenna climbed in.

"Yeah, you know how much I love cities."

Luke eased the car back into traffic. "So give me the full story on what happened here."

"Her roommate got shot—" Will began before feeling McKenna's glare burning holes through him.

"I can tell it myself. It's my case, remember?"

She'd seemed so out of it in the parking lot, he'd figured he'd step in. Apparently her independent streak objected.

She gave Luke a summary and by the time she'd finished they were pulling up in front of his apartment complex.

"I ordered Chinese. It should be here in a few minutes." Luke glanced at his watch. "Yep. Five minutes or so."

"Let's go inside and wait," Will urged both of them, not comfortable with McKenna being outside when her roommate had been a target such a short time before.

"I'm fine!" McKenna protested just as Luke said, "That was my plan—McKenna shouldn't be out in the open."

They headed toward the door. Will was pretty sure he saw McKenna roll her eyes at both of them as they fell into step near her, obviously keeping an eye on their surroundings.

McKenna might not agree, but clearly Will wasn't the only one who thought she needed protection.

* * *

If she'd thought Luke and Will were overly worried about her safety when she was a kid, she doubly thought so now.

They'd stopped her just inside the front door to the apartment and made her wait while Luke cleared all the rooms and closets and Will made sure the blinds were closed.

She wasn't ignoring the threat. It was hard to when it kept popping up everywhere. But they were overreacting.

"Anyone feel the need to test my food to make sure it's okay? The deliveryman could be trying to poison me," McKenna teased, holding out a forkful of General Tso's chicken.

Will grabbed the chicken between two fingers and popped it into his mouth. "Mmm."

"Seriously? You're worried about the food?"

Will laughed. "Nah. I just like that kind of chicken."

His laughter was contagious and she laughed along with him, swatting his hand. "No more food stealing."

"Hey, you offered it." Will shrugged and went back to his meal.

McKenna looked up. Luke was watching them, his eyebrows raised. She felt herself blush as she realized he'd seen their flirtatious exchange. Somehow she'd forgotten he was there.

She went back to eating and the guys eventually resumed the conversation they'd been having before the food arrived.

Her phone chirped just as she was finishing her meal. She glanced down at the screen and did a double take.

"It's a text message." McKenna blinked and swallowed hard. "From Anna's phone."

She saw Will tense as her thumb hovered over the button to bring it up and read it. Luke looked concerned, too, but his training allowed him to mask it better.

She clicked Open.

Your roommate learned her lesson about keeping her mouth shut. Next time, it's your turn.

He had her phone. The chill that began the moment she'd found Anna turned to ice.

Anna's near death hadn't been unconnected to McKenna.

It had been a deliberate message to McKenna. The threat against Anna had just gone from bad to worse.

McKenna dropped the phone as though it had burned her. "Call the hospital," she ordered Luke, Will, anyone listening. "Luke, don't you have some pull you can use up there? Anna's going to need a guard 24/7. Lexi and Matt, too." Frantic thoughts fought for her attention. "What else?"

Will grabbed her hands. "You have to calm down. Anna's going to be fine."

"Did you read it, Will? She was targeted on purpose!"

He tightened his grip on her hands. "Did *you* read it? He's focusing on you now. He's done with Anna. Whatever he thought she'd say, he's convinced she won't."

"Maybe because he thinks she's dead." They'd agreed it was best not to let anyone in Barrow know of Anna's condition, and to let people assume what they would, at least for now. McKenna thought the plan was a smart move on Lexi's part.

"For whatever reason, she's no longer a target. Nothing has happened this entire time she's been in the hospital. We're back to him being after you."

McKenna looked to Luke. He nodded, confirming what

Will had said. "Besides, your roommate is Anna *Richmond,* right?"

"Yeah. Why?"

Luke just stared. "You really didn't know?"

"Know what?"

"You've heard me talk about Captain Richmond. My boss. Right?"

"Yeah?" Feeling her patience, what little there had been to start with, waning, she was about to tell Luke to get on with it when she really thought about what he'd said. "Wait, Richmond? Are they related?"

"He's her dad. Trust me. She'll be well protected."

McKenna took a minute to absorb that information. It did explain a lot, like the fact that Anna hadn't been too fazed by the danger McKenna had worried she'd bring to her house. It also explained why Anna would have thought to invite McKenna on the midnight trip to the beach crime scene because it had looked as if it might be tied to her case.

"Oh," she finally said, nodding, wishing she didn't feel as though she'd suddenly lost all ability to speak.

"So she'll be fine," Luke finished, shaking his head. "That's weird she didn't say anything to you about it."

"I guess I did know her dad was in law enforcement somehow. Matt mentioned it once."

McKenna wasn't sure why it bothered her that she hadn't known. Maybe because she and Anna had been becoming better friends and it just seemed like the kind of information to share with a friend who was in the same line of work. But there was no need to dwell on that now. It really *wasn't* her business.

"That text message is important, though."

McKenna looked up at Luke, who'd spoken. "You said

Anna's safe. Obviously we know he's threatening me. Now we know he has her phone.... What else?"

"Pull it up and look again."

She did so. Your roommate learned her lesson about keeping her mouth shut. Next time, it's your turn.

"...keeping her mouth shut," she spoke aloud, adrenaline beginning to course through her. "So Anna knew something—something she might have planned to tell me."

Luke nodded. "I think so."

"But what? She wasn't even involved, as far as we know, right?" Will joined in.

McKenna shrugged. "I don't have the answers to those questions, either. Yet. But I'm going to find out."

"I have a feeling when you do, you'll have what you need to crack this case wide open."

TEN

The house looked exactly as McKenna had left it. Almost, anyway. There was crime scene tape everywhere. She knew it had been neatly put up yesterday, but today after hours of exposure to the harsh arctic winds, parts of it were tattered and hanging down, like something from a horror movie.

Okay, so the house looked nothing like she'd left it.

She let Mollie out of the car, keeping her on a leash to make sure she didn't escape. Will had dropped her off at his boss's house on their way out of town yesterday, assuring McKenna that his neighbor would be happy to watch her and would take good care of her. Checkers had flown to Anchorage with them yesterday and was staying with Anna's parents for the time being. Mollie seemed to miss her friend, but McKenna was glad she had only one animal to worry about right now.

She reached down to pet Mollie between the ears, noting how soft her fur was, as she tried to summon up the courage to go inside the house. Will had been right about his neighbor taking good care of her. She smelled like she'd had a bath.

"I guess it's not going to get easier," McKenna finally whispered to Mollie.

"Are we going in?"

Will's voice behind her started her. Again. She had to start doing a better job of paying attention to her surroundings. It was something they'd tried to drill into her mind at the trooper academy, and usually it stuck. But when she was stressed—ironic, since that was when she needed to be most alert—she tended to slip up.

"Might as well," she mumbled, forcing one foot in front of the other up the path to the front door. She slid her key in, deciding as a chill went through her that she was changing the locks. The police had found no evidence of a break-in, and while McKenna had a hard time believing someone Anna knew personally would have shot her, it was either that or believe that someone who wanted them both dead had a key to their house.

She shivered again. Yes, the locks were going to be one of the first things on her to-do list.

"Do you want me to go in first?" Will asked, concern lacing his tone. He'd been right there, every time she needed him, since they'd found Anna. Even though she'd insulted him—she saw that now—by suspecting one of his closest friends.

"I can do it," she said with more confidence than she felt. "And I'm sorry, Will. About suspecting…" She trailed off, suddenly mindful of how sound would carry in the cold air and knowing that anyone could be listening.

"I know."

"I don't suspect him anymore." Trusting Will should have been reason enough to take him off the list in the first place even before the killer targeted someone Matt would never hurt.

This case had to be solved before anyone else ended up in the hospital—or worse. But now she was starting to doubt her ability to find the culprit.

A voice echoed in her mind, reminding her that God was even more interested in justice than she was. But she couldn't think about God right now, not with thoughts of Anna's broken body still haunting the edges of her mind. God was a God of love. She knew that from what she'd been taught her whole life, and from what the Bible said. But He'd let Anna get hurt. Why?

McKenna didn't know.

She let Mollie off the leash and followed her into the house, more grateful than she was willing to admit that Will was following close behind her.

McKenna didn't know what she'd expected to feel when she reached her room and saw the aftermath of the attempted murder and investigation, but she felt nothing. It was as if she was watching the scene from somewhere outside herself.

None of her belongings had been disturbed. She hadn't been sure if the crime scene team would need to go through things or not. If they had, they'd been very careful to put everything back into place. Parts of the bloodstained carpet were missing, likely so they could take blood samples. Anna's blood was obviously there, but there was a chance the shooter's DNA could be there somewhere, too. A light layer of fingerprint dust covered several surfaces.

The air was stale and held a mix of smells McKenna couldn't identify, probably from the chemicals used to process the scene.

Her eyes drifted toward the dried pool of crimson.

"You're not staying here." Will said the words aloud just as she felt herself thinking them.

McKenna shrugged, hating the thought of sleeping in this house but not knowing what else to do.

"I'm serious. Stay at Matt and Lexi's. They're going to

be in Anchorage for a while anyway, with Anna. I know they wouldn't mind."

She was already shaking her head. "I think I've imposed on them enough, wouldn't you say? Staying with Lexi's sister and almost getting her killed?"

"That's not your fault, but we'll get into that more later. Right now I want your sleeping situation settled. Stay at my house if you'd rather do that, and I'll stay here."

McKenna tried in vain to pull her eyes from the mess on the floor, but it held her gaze as though magnetized and she found it almost impossible to look away. She swallowed hard. She wasn't going to take Will's house away, but she knew she had to give in somehow.

"Okay, I'll stay at their house if it'll make you stop pestering me."

"Good. I have a key. Just grab what you need for you and Mollie and we'll walk over there now."

McKenna wanted to protest. Really, she did. But the entire house felt tainted by what had happened. She didn't feel safe here. Not anymore.

"All right. Let's go."

McKenna slept on the foldout couch in Matt and Lexi's empty house that night. She dozed in and out of sleep all night, as did Mollie, who stayed on the floor beside her.

So many questions remained unanswered and plagued her through the dark predawn hours. Why had Anna been a target? Who was behind all this?

Maybe most important of all—when would it end?

McKenna must have fallen into a deeper sleep sometime around four, because when she opened her eyes again, the sun was shining and she felt surprisingly refreshed. She looked at the clock. Just past seven. She threw back the blanket she'd used to cover herself last night, patted the holster on her side to make sure her gun was still there and stood.

Today, she was going to find answers.

Her first stop was her office. She hadn't been by at all yesterday, since she'd left first thing to go out with Will and then come home to find Anna...the way she had. McKenna didn't know what she was looking for there, but it seemed like a good place to start. If all else failed, she'd call the guys at the crime lab in Anchorage and see if they could speed up the results of anything they'd discovered at the crime scene. Maybe Luke could call in a favor for her.

Although, if Luke was right about Anna's dad being a longtime officer there, the department was probably already doing everything they could to get results quickly.

She drove to the trooper station and let herself inside, feeling eyes on her the entire time she walked from her car to the door. Someone was watching her again. She was certain of that. But who? If it was the guy who wanted her dead, he would have shot her by now, right?

McKenna shut the door behind her the moment she'd stepped inside and bolted the locks. Then she let the blinds down, hoping the chills along her spine would go away if she knew no one could see her. They didn't, so she opened the blinds again, knowing it was probably smarter for her to be able to see out than to barricade herself in here.

First, she checked her office phone. No messages. Then the fax machine. Nothing there, either. It wasn't that she was expecting anything, but she'd thought she'd better check in case Captain Wilkins had stumbled upon a lead he wanted to pass on.

McKenna sat down at the desk with a notepad in front of her as she tried to collect her thoughts.

What she wanted to do today was figure out who'd shot Anna. But technically, that wasn't her job. The North

Slope Bureau Police Department would be investigating the shooting, in conjunction with the state crime lab in Anchorage. One of the officers had flown with them to Anchorage yesterday to hear McKenna's story of finding Anna. Just because McKenna's gut instinct told her that Anna's shooting was linked to her case didn't meant it was. The text message she'd gotten from Anna's cell yesterday seemed to imply that, but even that wasn't solid evidence. Anyone could have that phone. The text could be a prank. Stranger things had happened.

Maybe she could work to establish a link between her dead hunters case and Anna's shooting. That would give her an opening to help bring her roommate's attacker to justice. First, she'd email Captain Wilkins and bring him up-to-date on what had happened with Anna and her thoughts on that. She turned the computer on and waited. The ancient desktop finally found the motivation to fully power on. McKenna opened her email program.

And found a new email from Anna.

Her stomach rolled as she worried it might be another note from her would-be murderer. Then she checked the date and time on the message. It was sent yesterday morning. Not long after McKenna had missed the call from Anna on her cell when she was out with Will.

Heart racing, she opened the email.

McKenna, I decided I can't wait to talk to you in person. I'm not sure if it's the best idea to talk about this over email, which is why I'm sending it to your work address. More secure, right? Bad news first, I think someone may have followed me from the clinic. Now for what may be good news. I got called in to treat injuries George received in a fight earlier this morning.

McKenna tensed. George had been in a fight? Was it the fight with Will, when he tried to shoot her? Or was the timing wrong, clearing him from suspicion?

While I was checking out his injuries, he was mumbling things about hunters stealing from the land, about troopers not managing it well…his usual rant. But what caught my attention this time is that he said something about the polar bear population being low this year. He thinks someone is hunting polar bears, but that doesn't make sense. Only natives can do that legally, right? Aren't they a protected species?

I'm sending this from my phone. I'm on my way home. I pulled over into a parking lot to type this when you didn't answer your phone, and my battery is low so I have to go now. Save this email if you need it because I have my phone set to delete any message that I send, including this one. You should be home soon, so I'll see you then. Your turn to cook tonight? Or is Will bringing us food?

She shivered at the end of the message. Anna couldn't have sent this long before someone shot her. There was something eerie in knowing that life had been going on normally and then…not.

McKenna reread the message. It was too coincidental that all of that had happened the day Anna was shot. She shivered again, but this time from anticipation. She was relatively certain she had one of her answers right here.

Anna was shot because of her conversation with George.

But how had the shooter known what they'd talked about? And why did it matter to him? Why would someone care if she knew the polar bear population was low? Unless someone *was* hunting illegally.

Then why not shoot George for talking? But then, who

would take the comments of a bitter old drunk seriously…
unless they were backed by someone credible who believed
him. Like Anna.

Her mind took another track. Was it possible George
was behind it all? He could have been drunk, maybe, and
said too much to Anna and then needed to silence her.

Neither option was good.

Both options gave her something to look into.

This case was heating back up in a hurry. McKenna
printed a copy of the email for her files, closed down the
computer and called Will.

She needed to go check on the polar bear population.
But first, she needed to talk to the man who was more and
more becoming her top person of interest.

"I want to know what you know about polar bear poaching." McKenna wasted no time coming to the point when
George answered his door. If he was surprised, it didn't
show on the lines etched in his leathery face. He just stood
there with the door partially open, staring at her. McKenna's heart beat a quick rhythm in her chest as she second-
guessed her decision to come alone—maybe she should
have taken Will up on his offer to come. But as incompetent as George seemed to think troopers were to begin
with, she didn't want to reinforce that perception by bringing civilian "backup."

"I'm not sure what you mean."

"You talked to Anna about it yesterday," she countered.

This time an expression crossed his face. McKenna
couldn't quite identify the emotions behind it but it was
there. She was definitely on to something.

He narrowed his eyes, his look becoming more con-
temptuous by the minute. "If you mean the paramedic who
patched me up—" he motioned to the bruises on his face

and on one arm "—then yes, I talked to her. But I don't know why that would interest you."

McKenna clenched her jaw, taking deep breaths to calm her temper, but it wasn't working. Every time she started to feel as if her emotions were under control, she thought of Anna. Saw her lying on the floor, helpless. "This isn't a game, George," she said in a low tone, hoping to remove that look of condescension from his face. "People are dying and I need to know why."

"Greed, most likely. Those people are always greedy."

"You keep saying that. *Those* people. Who are *those* people? And what do you know about the low polar bear population? Are *you* killing them?" She knew it wasn't exactly the questioning progression they taught at the trooper academy, but it was the best she could do at the moment. Maybe her to-the-point questions would shake him up, make him give her some straight answers.

He stared at her for the space of several heartbeats. "Even if I was killing them…" He leveled her with a glare. "You couldn't stop me. Native Alaskans are allowed to harvest polar bears, responsibly, for subsistence reasons. Or didn't you know that, Miss *Wildlife* Trooper?"

"I'm aware of the laws. I'm also aware that there are tagging and reporting requirements and if you're not meeting those for one reason or another, you're guilty of committing a crime."

Her heart thudded in her chest as George regarded her.

"Always suspecting the wrong people. Assuming things." He shook his head.

"I'm not trying to assume. I'm trying to solve this!" She couldn't keep the earnest desperation from her tone. Again, showing so much emotion was something she feared might be hurting her investigative abilities, but she was way more emotionally invested in this case than she'd ever thought she'd be when she went through training.

George watched her. Said nothing. Then finally spoke.

"East of town," he said slowly, in a quiet voice, "the polar bear population seems to have dropped. They've been dropping for some time now, but I am growing more and more concerned." He narrowed his eyes again. "Isn't it your job to keep track of that?"

As if she could be held personally responsible for tracking the hundreds of thousands of individual animals of all different species in her area—on her second week at the job. "It's *part* of my job, yes."

"If you want to do it well, I suggest you look into that. That is all. I have nothing else to say to you." In one motion, George stepped backward into the house and slammed the door.

Apparently, their conversation was over.

McKenna looked down at the ground to gather her thoughts, then looked back up, glancing around as she ran back to her car. She needed to contact Will, fast, and get a flight out to the east of Barrow.

Anna hadn't had much time from when she had the same conversation with George to when he or someone else had come after her. McKenna wasn't going to waste whatever time she did have. She was getting closer. And one way or another, she was going to beat the clock and finish this.

As she climbed into her car, she realized she hadn't felt as if she was being watched during her conversation with George. Coincidence? Or was he the one who'd been watching her?

ELEVEN

Will did a final check of his plane and glanced at his watch again. McKenna was meeting him at the airport in five minutes. She hadn't said much when she texted, just told him she needed him and asked if he could meet her with the plane ready to go.

He'd needed a destination so he could file a flight plan and he'd finally managed to get that info out of her, but that was all. She'd been adamant about not talking about it on the phone.

So for now he was planning a flight along the coast, not knowing exactly why. The things a man would do for a woman.

He walked back to the cockpit and climbed in, deciding he may as well wait for her in there.

She came running across the runway three minutes later, waving her arms at him.

"Go, go, go!" she shouted as she climbed in and slammed the door.

The events of the last week all too clear in his mind, he took off without question, taxiing across the runway and then lifting off in one seamless, effortless motion.

Once they were in the air and at their cruising altitude, he glanced her way. "Mind telling me what that is all about?"

"Someone's been following me all day." She cocked her head to the side. "Well, not all day. I didn't notice it when I was at George's house."

She said the words casually, as if she was telling him what she'd had for breakfast that morning. "Someone's following you and you didn't call me? And why were you at George's house *alone?* I thought when you turned down my offer to go with you that you'd changed your mind about going."

"I did call you—well, I texted you—just now. And I was alone because it's my job." She frowned at him, head titled to the side in that adorable way she had when she thought he was being overprotective.

Wait. Adorable? When had he let that be an acceptable way to describe her in his mind? Wasn't he trying to fight this crazy feeling of intense attraction? He had to think of her as Luke's little sister. As someone completely, thoroughly, wrong for him.

If he didn't, he'd soon run out of good reasons not to admit his feelings for her.

"This is the first I'm hearing of someone following you."

"Oh. I didn't call you about the stalker. That's true. But I did call to ask you for help. See? I know when I need help. I'm making progress."

Her grin was too cute to lecture her. At the moment. So he decided to let it go for the time being. Until the word she'd used came back and startled him. "Stalker? We've gone from someone following you to stalker?"

"It's really the same thing."

"Stalker implies a little more intensity, McKenna." Were they seriously having this conversation? "And why were you at George's house?"

"Okay, let me explain." She settled back against the seat. "These seats are super comfortable."

"Thanks. Now, focus. The stalker? George?"

"I've wondered several times since I got to Barrow if someone was following me. It actually happened the first night I was in town, before I'd even started work. I wrote it off as paranoia. Then when everything happened, I started to pay closer attention, but I was never sure. Today I *knew* someone was watching me. Like I said, I didn't notice it at George's house. But just in case, I took a complicated route to the airstrip to try to lose him if he was there and I didn't notice." She shrugged. "But I don't know how good of a stalker he is."

"You sound entirely too laid-back about this." It was like having a conversation with her brother, who would talk casually about crime scenes and then shift the conversation to sports without a second thought, as though they were both equally normal subjects to discuss.

"Think about it, Will. If the stalker were the same person as the guy who's after me, he would have tried to kill me by now."

"Someone *has* been trying to kill you. In case that has somehow escaped your notice."

"Yes." She glared at him, as if he was the one being unreasonable. "Thank you. I did notice that." She waved a hand dismissively. "But no one has tried to kill me when I've felt like someone is watching me. Besides, I went to my office alone this morning—early, before there were many people out. I was an easy target."

McKenna said the words as if she was trying to make him feel better, but somehow they just didn't have the desired effect.

He hoped his glare told her so.

"And in answer to your other question, I was at George's house to get information. And I think I struck gold."

"How's that?"

"He does know something about the polar bear population. Anna was right. All I could get out of him was that the population is dwindling, and that I should look to the east of town."

"What do you mean, she was right?"

"I didn't tell you about the email? She sent me an email, just before she was shot, about George telling her the polar bear population outside of town seemed low. She wondered if that could tie into the case somehow. And I think she was right."

"So, do you still think George is behind it all even though he seems to be helping you?"

She frowned. "I don't know. He could be. This could be a trap."

Great. That was reassuring.

"Or he could be genuinely concerned about the animals." She looked off into the distance. "It's getting harder to narrow down who I can trust. I have feelings about different people, but I don't know how much I should trust my instincts."

He identified with that problem completely. About this case and about his relationship with McKenna.

Coincidently enough, when they flew over the stretch of coastline McKenna wanted to investigate, they saw a beached whale.

"Jackpot," she breathed. "Perfect polar bear bait. How close to that whale can you land this thing?"

Will frowned. "Do you want to check the bear population? Or get eaten by it?"

"All right. Just pay attention to landmarks. Wherever we do land, we're going to need to hike back here."

Will had never been so thankful for the .44-caliber revolver he kept on his belt when he was flying. There were few animals out here that made him truly nervous, but the polar bear was known for its brutality. It was the only bear species in Alaska that would deliberately hunt down and eat a human for any other reason than utter starvation.

He guided the plane down to a flat spot by a small river, probably a mile away from the coast. "Does this work for you?"

McKenna patted the boots on her feet. "I came prepared for a hike. We'll be fine."

They climbed out of the airplane and Will did his postflight check. "All right, Sherlock," he teased McKenna. "Lead the way."

She laughed as she started across the tundra in the direction of the ocean. "Maybe I seem a little melodramatic today, but it's because this case is finally showing some signs of progress. We're close. I can feel it."

So could he.

As they approached the whale carcass, which was more of a skeleton at this point, the first thing Will noticed was the stench. It was unlike anything he'd smelled, even with all his hunting experience.

McKenna gagged. "Why polar bears would eat that, I have no idea, but usually they love it." She looked around. "But I don't see any." She shivered a little. "How many do you think are watching us, though?"

The landscape where they were didn't leave many places for an animal that large to hide, which was a small consolation. But Will could see that McKenna's tip had been right. If this area was as populated with polar bears as it should be, even now that the whale was down to bones, bears would be feasting on it.

The fact that they weren't said they all had plenty to eat

already. Which said that there were fewer bears than usual sharing this area and fighting over the food.

"I think you found a motive strong enough for murder." He looked back at McKenna. "If someone is hunting polar bears illegally, they might kill to keep that information hidden."

The offense was a serious one. Whoever was behind this would go down, in a big way, if he was caught, facing heavy fines and possibly jail time. Which meant he had nothing to lose.

"Let's get back to the plane." Will heard the tension in his voice. Chills ran down his spine as he realized it wasn't only polar bears that could conceivably be hiding and watching them. And it was the two-legged human predators that could be there, sniper rifles trained on them, that he was more concerned with.

He expected her to argue.

She didn't.

The wind sounded as though it was crying as it moaned through the tundra. McKenna couldn't blame it. The things that had happened here if they were right—polar bears illegally killed, people murdered... If she were the wind and had seen it all, she'd cry, too.

Why did people do evil things? It didn't matter how long she did this kind of work, how many stories she heard from Luke about the depravity of humanity, she would never understand. And maybe that was good. She was pretty sure she wouldn't *want* to understand.

Becoming a wildlife trooper had been something she'd wanted to do to help. To keep animals safe, and bring justice down on the people who broke the laws related to them. Never had she dreamed she'd be seeking justice for crimes done to people, something even more important, but even more emotionally draining.

McKenna continued hiking, glancing over her shoulder to make sure Will was still there.

"I'm here," he assured her.

There were days she loved this land, days that even though she'd rather live in a city, she relished the vast expanse of nothing. The wild, stunning beauty that was Alaska.

Today it haunted her, chilled her to the core. The plane couldn't come in sight fast enough.

When they finally reached it, McKenna climbed inside, shivering though it wasn't cold. She sat alone while Will did his inspection, trying to wrap her mind around the wispy threads of this case that all seemed to be coming together.

Someone had been killing polar bears illegally. Then two bodies had ended up on the tundra, and it seemed the two incidents were connected. Had the victims found out about the polar bear hunting and threatened to expose whoever was behind it? Had *they* been behind it? Maybe, but if so, they hadn't been acting alone. A killer was still out there—the man who had attacked her and nearly killed Anna.

Who was responsible?

She had suspects, but no concrete evidence pointing solidly at any of them. She had to look deeper.

God, if you really are interested in the outcome of this case, please help me, she prayed, realizing even as she thought the words that He had. What were the chances they'd come across a dead whale, the perfect "bait" for polar bears, which would make it easy to check on the population in this area?

Maybe He cared a little after all.

"Ready to go?" Will asked as he climbed in and readied the plane for takeoff, fiddling with buttons and knobs on the instrument panel.

"Yes."

He took off smoothly, guiding them back up into the air with the skill of someone who spent more time behind the throttle of a plane than the wheel of a car.

"I don't know what to think," she confessed as they flew over the scene they'd just investigated. "George was telling the truth. But does that mean he's behind it and that's how he knew for sure? Or does it mean he's innocent, and is trying to help with the case?"

"I don't know what motive he'd have for telling you if he was guilty." Will shrugged. "Unless he feels confident you won't find any evidence pointing to him and he's trying to taunt you."

He did seem like that kind of person. But was that reaching too far for answers? The most logical conclusion would seem to be that he wasn't responsible for the murders and the poaching. But then, who was?

McKenna relaxed against the seat again—they really were so comfortable—and closed her eyes. The flight back to Barrow wasn't too long, but maybe she'd catch a quick nap before they got back. Then she could jump into the case with both feet again. Her brain was on overload at the moment, and any attempts to synthesize the information were falling short.

She hadn't been asleep for long, if she'd fallen asleep at all, when the entire body of the plane jolted, startling her eyes open. "What was that?" she asked Will, half expecting him to tease her about overreacting.

The tight set of his jaw made her stomach churn. "I don't know," he said, not taking his eyes off the instrument panel and the glass in front of the plane. He looked at all the readouts then scanned the horizon.

"You're not, like, looking for somewhere to land, are you?" she asked, again thinking she must be overreacting.

Will didn't answer. He didn't have a chance, because the plane jolted again, the entire body shuddering, stuck in some kind of terrifying convulsion, before she heard a loud noise and the engine seemed to lose power.

"Will?"

"Just hang on!" he yelled over the deafening quiet. The cabin of the plane that had hummed with activity and a thousand different working parts just minutes earlier was now silent.

McKenna was no pilot, but she was pretty sure that was a bad sign. She double-checked her seat belt and gripped the armrests on either side of her seat as tightly as she could.

But really, what good was holding on going to do her while they fell out of the sky in a tiny metal box with wings from twenty thousand feet?

As the plane fell, she had a surprising amount of time to think, more than she would have guessed. She thought about her relationship with God, how maybe there could have been more there than she'd allowed there to be. She thought about her family, about Luke and her parents and how much she'd miss them even when they got on her nerves. She thought about her job, briefly wrestled with the knowledge that she'd never have the chance to keep moving up as she'd dreamed of doing.

And then she thought about Will. How she loved him and had always been too afraid to say so.

She wasn't afraid now. Not now that they were both about to die. But the words wouldn't come. Her mouth was sealed shut as much as her eyes were being held open, forced to watch the brown and green of the ground approach faster than it ever should from an airplane.

McKenna braced herself for the impact, wondering if it would hurt, if she'd be in pain for long before the end came.

The only thing she didn't wonder about was if she was going to die. Because that was what happened to people whose planes crashed, right? As far as she knew, crashing meant certain death. From any altitude.

The plane shattered as it hit the ground. McKenna felt the impact. And then nothing.

TWELVE

"McKenna?" As soon as he'd blinked enough times to clear his head, Will turned his head to where McKenna had sat in the passenger seat. It was empty. He'd landed the plane the best he could, softening the impact, but his skills hadn't been enough to overcome whatever had gone wrong.

And McKenna may have paid for his inadequacies.

Panic grabbed him as he took in the broken glass all over the seat and realized she must have been tossed from the plane. He fumbled with his seat belt, wondering if hers had broken in the crash. "McKenna!" He pushed at the door, but it wouldn't budge. Wincing, he bent his arm and used his elbow to slam against the door.

It opened and he climbed out, running to her side of the plane, scanning the ground as he did so and praying that he'd find her relatively unhurt.

Was that too much to ask for with how bad the crash had been? It was amazing enough that he was unhurt except for a small scratch on his forearm.

He scanned the scene, hoping he was looking for someone with minor injuries and not for a body. "McKenna?" he called again. He stepped over a piece of metal that had come from somewhere on his plane, hardly flinching at the damage that had been inflicted on his most prized possession. The plane didn't matter as much as McKenna did.

Short of his relationship with God, nothing did.

Will's breath caught in his throat and he tried to slow his heart rate as the realization he was in love with her, probably always had been somewhere in his heart, washed over him with the certainty of a tsunami.

She had to be okay.

"McKenna!" he yelled again.

A weak voice somewhere to his right grabbed his attention. "McKenna, is that you?" he asked. *Of course it was her, who else would it be?* He hurried toward the sound and found her lying there, pinned beneath some of the cargo he kept in his plane for emergencies.

"I see you found my first-aid kit," he teased once he looked her over and saw that she was relatively unharmed. Relief flooded through him and his heart returned to a normal pace.

"You're okay," she said, and he saw the expression on her face begin to mirror the overwhelming relief he was certain was on his own. He had no reason to believe her feelings went as far as his own, but she clearly cared for him deeply. It was a start.

"I'm fine. How are you, really?"

"I'm good. I can't believe it, but I'm okay. Except that I'm stuck."

After looking more closely at where the large box pinned her leg down, making sure nothing had punctured her leg anywhere—he knew it would be foolish to remove anything that had because he'd be putting her in danger of losing too much blood—Will wrestled the large container out of the way.

McKenna looked down at her leg and flexed her foot a few times. "I think I'm okay now."

"Good." He reached down a hand to help her up. She took it willingly and stood, though she faltered after the first step she tried to take. "Easy, easy," he coached, and she nodded her agreement as she stood still for a minute, letting her body recover from the accident and from being stuck in one place for so long.

"So what happened?" she finally asked. Will followed her gaze back to the remains of the plane, his heart now free to mourn its loss since McKenna was okay. His knowledge of mechanics was just basic enough to fix common problems on the airplane if it needed it, but not detailed enough to know for sure if what he feared was true or not. But he worried the plane was beyond repair.

"I'm not sure," he said slowly, his mind having worked on that question since the moment he'd lost control and they'd started falling out of the sky like a child's toy airplane.

"But you checked everything." She met his eyes, hers tinged with fear. "I watched you."

He nodded. "I know."

"So that could only mean…"

"Sabotage." The word tasted bad in his mouth as he said it out loud. It was the only explanation he'd been able to come up with. He'd tried others. In some ways he even wished carelessness on his part had caused the crash. If that was the case, he'd feel terrible for endangering McKenna, but it would mean she was safer, that someone didn't want her dead badly enough to go to the trouble of disabling his plane and trying to kill them both.

As it was, he had no choice but to admit that whoever was after her was not going to stop. Not as long as she was still alive.

His heart thudded hard and he swallowed, willing himself not to give away any of his feelings. She was scared enough already.

"Of all the…"

Will heard a loud clank and looked down in time to see a piece of metal skid across the ground as McKenna withdrew her foot.

"Did you kick that?"

She looked up at him through narrowed eyes. "Yes." Her expression practically dared him to do something about it.

"It's a crime scene now, McKenna," he reminded her gently.

Her eyes widened and the fight in them disappeared as tears began to pool.

In all their years of knowing each other, he'd rarely seen her cry. This was twice in one week. The only other time he remembered seeing her cry was the time she'd broken her leg when she was five.

"Why can't I do this right?" Her lip quivered as she sank to the ground, hugging her knees to her as tears spilled over.

He knelt beside her. "It's okay. Really." He watched her shoulders shake, not sure what he should do, not sure what she *wanted* him to do. When he could take it no more, he moved closer to her, wrapped his arms around her and pulled her close. "It's going to be okay."

He held her as she cried until her muffled sobs seemed to slow.

"I just…" She sniffed and brushed a tear from her cheek as though she was irritated by its presence. And knowing her, she probably was. "I just don't know what I should be doing differently. I don't think like a cop the same way Luke does, Will. I graduated from the trooper academy just like any other trooper, but all my experience is with wildlife. I *know* wildlife." She threw up her hands. "And if all of this is related to the polar bear poaching, I think I can solve it eventually, but how many people will be killed by then?" Her expression sobered further. "You could have died today. Because of me."

"No. Not because of you. I got myself into this on purpose."

"Because of me."

Seeing he wasn't going to be able to change her mind on this, Will fell silent.

"Do you have a SAT phone or anything we could use to call for help?" she asked a minute later.

He nodded. "I've got one…" He let his voice trail off.

"But?"

"I'd rather not use it just yet. Let's give it until tomorrow, see if anyone comes looking for us. We'll use it if we need it, but I'd rather not broadcast our location in case whoever's after you finds it out and comes to finish the job."

He could tell by the uncertain expression on her face that neither option sat well with her. He understood. It was hard to know which one was best—he'd been debating it himself. This option, though, waiting it out for the rest of the day, seemed like the best one.

"I really need to let Captain Wilkins know what's going on." She gestured to the mess around them.

Will understood. He really did. But he still believed keeping the SAT phone off was best, at least for now.

"We'll call as soon as we can."

McKenna nodded.

"For now, let's set up camp. It'll keep us safer out here." It would also give them something to do, maybe keep shock from setting in. Will worried about the look in McKenna's eyes. She was a fighter, but this wasn't the kind of fight she was used to. He could already see the stress of the case, the violence of it, taking its toll on her.

How much longer could she hold out? Would it be long enough to keep her alive?

"One of us should try to get some sleep," Will said, nudging her arm. "You can have a turn first."

She shook her head, the idea of being alone not appealing to her at all. "I'm fine. I'd rather sit up, if that's okay."

Will leaned forward and built the fire up a little more, then sat back. "We'll sit and talk, then. Pretend we're on some kind of date." He laughed as he said the words.

That laughter reminded McKenna why she could never admit what she felt for him. She couldn't take the thought of him laughing at her feelings, and if he had any idea, she was sure he would. After all, she was Luke's little sister. And she was the opposite of him in almost every way. He loved being out here, in the middle of nowhere. She enjoyed the outdoors, but would rather make her permanent home somewhere within easy driving distance of gourmet coffee and a large grocery store.

Not that either of those things was that big of a deal. No, one of the biggest obstacles was the fact that she liked her life neat and controlled. Will was too laid-back for that. The two of them together would never work out. And then what would happen to their friendship?

She was afraid she knew. And since she couldn't guarantee what would happen, it was definitely better to keep things the way they were.

"Like that would ever happen, though, right?" She knew she shouldn't even joke about it, shouldn't open a door to that conversation. But part of her wanted to know what Will's reaction would be. She chanced a look at his face and saw an expression she wasn't sure how to define.

Butterflies twirled in her stomach. McKenna cleared her throat, feeling closer to him than she had in years and desperately needing to do something, anything, to bring herself back to earth. The weird feelings she was having were because her emotions were crazy in the post-crash stress. Those, mixed with an old crush that she never could quite extinguish, could create a dangerous combination. "So…we really are in the middle of nowhere, aren't we?"

Will nodded, his smile widening with every breath of the fresh, uncivilized air. McKenna exhaled. Change of subject complete.

"You have to admit, being out in God's creation like this, it's not so bad."

"It is pretty out here," McKenna admitted. "It would be easier to enjoy if we hadn't crashed an airplane to get here, though."

Will studied her face for a minute. "That's something you've always struggled with, isn't it?"

"What?" She felt herself tensing. The change of subject was supposed to have gotten them on to a less serious conversation. It felt in some ways as if they were headed into deeper waters than they'd been in earlier when she'd panicked.

"Not appreciating things you didn't plan."

"I don't do that."

"No?" He shook his head, a gentle smile easing the blow of his next words, but only slightly. "You just said yourself that it's pretty here. If we'd come here on purpose and built a fire, just to enjoy being outside, being together, wouldn't you be happy?"

She said nothing. But she didn't need to. Will knew her better than that, knew he was right.

"It's because you didn't plan it that it bothers you. The

plane crash was out of your control. Being stuck here is out of your control. And that makes you uncomfortable."

There were times when, though it was opposite from her personality, Will's laid-back take on life was enjoyable to McKenna. Refreshing, even. But right now it was just making the frustration that had been building since the moment they started to fall out of the sky build to its exploding point.

Yet another difference between them that made anything more than friendship a bad idea.

"I can't be uncomfortable about a plane crash caused by someone trying to kill me? You know what? Maybe I'm not the only one with a struggle. Nothing is a big deal to you, Will. You just take life as it comes and roll with it. Just because some of us have a greater sense of responsibility for what happens to us and to those around us doesn't make it wrong."

"Plenty of things are a big deal to me." His voice was low and calm. "I never said you were the only one who had a hard time dealing with situations outside of human control."

"You're talking about Rachael," McKenna realized aloud. "Like I told you the other day—"

"I know." He nodded. "You were right. In my head, I know that her death wasn't my fault. God is the one in control. I still struggle to accept that in my heart, but I'm working on it. All I'm saying is that maybe you need to start working on it, too."

McKenna shifted closer to the warmth of the fire. "I don't disagree with you about God being in control."

"Not with your words."

She glared at him. "I'm the one whose shoulders this case rests on."

"Not God's?"

McKenna threw up her hands. "I know God's in control, Will! But He doesn't seem to be doing anything about this case, which means it's really up to me."

"I think you know better than that."

"Yeah, well…" McKenna poked at the fire with a piece of metal from the airplane, since sticks weren't overly abundant in the middle of the grassy tundra. "Speaking of the case…" She hoped he wouldn't call her out on yet another change of subject. "Any ideas about who did this?" She motioned to the remains of Will's plane.

He grimaced. "Probably the same person who wants you dead."

"But how did he know I was going to call you today and ask for you to fly me somewhere?" She shook her head. "How many people even know how to sabotage airplanes? If it was me, I wouldn't know where to start—especially if it had to be sabotage that wouldn't show up on a standard check by the pilot. It doesn't make sense."

"I don't know. Lots of people around here have a pilot's license and experience, but I don't have a clue who would do this. In all the years I've been in Barrow, nothing like this has happened. Most of the crime is alcohol related, usually domestic violence. What about you? Any suspicions?"

She took a deep breath and searched her mind, feeling as if she was grasping for puzzle pieces that weren't there. "I don't know. I'm not even sure who I can eliminate from the suspect pool."

"Besides Matt."

McKenna shrugged. "He's off the list now. So I guess we're back to George and Chris as my main suspects. Though I have to say, I'm not sure I was completely wrong to suspect Matt."

"I thought you said—"

"I misspoke. That's not what I meant." There he went, getting defensive again. What would it be like to be someone he cared enough about to defend like that?

"What I meant," McKenna went on, "is that I suspected him partially because his job makes him a prime candidate, especially now that we know the polar bear poaching ties in. Which is why I'm wondering about Rick now."

"So you're basing suspects on the fact that they hunt?"

"No, not just that. But he owns his own hunting company. He's familiar with planes, which we now know is part of the profile. He would have had opportunity, and potentially motive."

"Motive?"

"Illegal hunts pay well."

"Rick's never done anything illegal that I know of." He didn't sound convinced by her logic.

She shrugged. "It still makes sense. Are you saying you trust Rick, that you'd vouch for him like you did Matt?"

"I wouldn't say that." He paused. "But I wouldn't say I'd easily believe he's a criminal, either. He's not always the best boss, but I've never known him to be deliberately dishonest."

"Which is more than we can say for George."

"Has he lied to you?"

"Yes and no." She made a face. "There's more to the story of what happened to that guy on the beach that he wasn't telling. I don't know if he's lying to protect himself because he's guilty, or because he doesn't want to cooperate with an organization he's opposed to."

"I see."

"I just wish it made sense. I wish I could be sure about something and wrap this up. This is my job. I'm supposed to be good at it."

"You're doing the best you can."

"That's not enough. People are getting seriously hurt and dying."

"But like I said, God is still in control. Trust Him."

He said it as if it was the easiest thing in the world. She felt her defenses rise again, but this time she didn't have the fight left to verbally defend herself. Instead, she took a deep breath. "I think we'd better talk about something else."

Several heartbeats of silence passed. "You know what?" Will began.

Something in his tone sent shivers of anticipation through McKenna. "What?"

"I've missed you these past few years. And while I would have picked different circumstances, I'm glad to be here with you, spending time with you like this again."

She felt her face warm. "Thanks."

"You're welcome." He glanced down at his watch. "We've still got a few hours until morning. Sure you don't want to get some sleep?"

"I'm sure."

"Okay, so what should we talk about next?"

"This reminds me of sitting with you on the rocks by Resurrection Bay. Looking up at the stars, talking about anything…" She'd always had a crush on him, but that summer she'd lost her heart to him entirely, and she was relatively certain he'd never even known.

"That was one of my favorite summers. One of the best times of my life, really." He smiled at her but she didn't smile back.

"Hey." He touched her hand lightly. "What's wrong?"

"After all the time we spent together that summer, I thought you'd write me that following year," McKenna admitted softly.

Will sighed. "You were…you were amazing. And it felt like you knew me, really knew me like no one ever had."

She listened to the crackling of the fire, waiting for his next words, bracing herself for the sting of rejection they'd certainly carry with them.

"But you were also…"

She finished for him. "Luke's little sister."

He nodded, smiling a sad smile tinged with regret. "Yeah."

Several more minutes went by. McKenna alternated between watching the fire burn in front of her and looking out across the vastness of the tundra, gathering up the courage for her next words. "If—" She stopped.

"If what?" His voice deepened.

"I hadn't been his little sister…" She looked up to meet Will's eyes, watched the fire's reflection dance in their depths.

A crack somewhere behind them broke the silence of the night.

Will jerked away from McKenna, not sure why he'd been leaning closer to her in the first place. "It came from that way."

She nodded. "I think you're right."

Will glanced in that direction, then back at McKenna. The tundra ground wasn't overly dry, but the idea of leaving an unattended fire, even for a short time, made him nervous.

"I'll stay by the fire," McKenna offered, seeming to read his mind. Will nodded his thanks and moved away from their makeshift camp toward where he'd heard the noise, gun unholstered and ready in case he met with trouble. He kept every sense on high alert as he surveyed the area as best he could in the darkness. Everything seemed quiet now. Overly hushed in the wake of the noise they'd heard that had broken up...whatever it had broken up.

He crept quietly over the tundra grass, determined to make sure there was no danger lurking before he went back to McKenna.

McKenna. She had always been special to him. But Will had always prided himself on his ability to look at their friendship logically, and realize it wouldn't do either of them any good to pursue a relationship deeper than what they already had.

Although that plane crash today—the thought that had plagued him when he couldn't find her, the idea that she might not have been okay—did crazy things to his mind.

He crept through the darkness for another few minutes, shining his flashlight at anything that might merit a second look. Nothing. Of course, Will knew if an animal had caused the noise, it had likely disappeared and hidden itself somewhere by now.

Will turned around, back toward their camp. As he approached the glow of the fire, he turned to where McKenna had been sitting. "I guess it was just an animal—" he began.

McKenna wasn't there.

"McKenna?" He kept his voice steady, level, even, as he tried to will his heartbeat to do the same. She'd probably just walked off for a minute. Maybe she'd gone to sleep. With swift footsteps, he checked the entire area around their campsite.

He didn't see her anywhere.

"McKenna!" he called louder, turning three hundred and sixty degrees as he squinted into the darkness, tried to make out any sign of her. There were hundreds of thousands of acres of wilderness in all directions. Searching for her when he didn't have an inkling of where to start was a bad idea, but standing there and doing nothing while she was missing had his stomach twisting in knots.

His muscles tightened and his heart started to pound as he stood and listened to the night sounds. Years of living in the wilderness had taught him that it wasn't always effective to go after something right away. Sometimes you had to be patient, give it time. Listen.

A rustle to his right was all it took for him to run in that direction.

And run straight into McKenna.

"Will!" she yelled, sounding more irritated than terrified as she gripped his shoulders with both hands, struggling not to lose her footing.

Alive. She was alive. Feelings he couldn't identify threatened to overwhelm him, so Will did the only thing that made logical sense in that emotionally charged moment.

He pulled McKenna toward him and claimed her lips in a kiss.

McKenna's heart raced as she lifted her lips to meet his. She returned his kiss with what felt like all the dreams she'd been storing up for years. It was perfect…until at the same moment, both of them seemed to realize what they were doing and pulled away from each other.

McKenna's eyes locked with Will's. They stood that way for at least a minute. Staring. Their eyes asking questions of each other that neither seemed able to answer.

Will was the one to finally break the silence. He cleared his throat. "There's no one out there. I think we heard some kind of animal, but there were no obvious tracks, so it must have been small."

His warm voice made her feel as if she was wrapped up in her favorite blanket, a mug of hot coffee in hand.

She wanted to snuggle back up next to him and pick up where they'd left off. But from the distance he was carefully maintaining between them, that option apparently wasn't on the table.

"You really should probably turn in now." Will nudged her shoulder in a brotherly way. "There's no sense in both of us keeping watch all night. We can take turns."

She swallowed hard. She knew she hadn't imagined the sparks between them, that just minutes ago had been as real as the ones that danced in the fire. But maybe Will had only been overwhelmed by the fact that she was okay. He'd seemed nervous when he couldn't find her, which McKenna supposed made sense. She'd just needed to slip away to relieve herself, but could see why her not being at the fire when he returned would have made Will panic.

That explained his half of the kiss anyway. And what of the passion with which she'd kissed him back? Surely a childhood crush couldn't still feel like *that*. Will was probably embarrassed, wondering what she'd been thinking, responding the way she had. "I guess you're right," McKenna finally agreed, waiting for him to say something, anything, that indicated he understood the gravity of what had passed between them.

"Get some good sleep, McKenna." His face was serious, full of horribly *brotherly* concern. "I have a feeling this is just going to get worse before it gets better. There's a blanket in my emergency kit. Feel free to use that." He turned to the fire to stoke it. It roared back to life under his attention.

"Okay." McKenna nodded, though he couldn't see her now with his back to her, accepting his dismissal. So he was going to act as if the kiss had never happened? Fine. She could play along with that. It was for the best, anyway.

She reached for the blanket he'd mentioned and laid it

down on the ground. She also found a Bible in the emergency kit. It wasn't something she would have thought to put in a kit like this one, but it was like Will to think of it. She smiled. It said something about the genuineness of his faith that this book would be something he would want around when there was trouble.

McKenna laid down on the blanket and stared up at the dark sky. She closed her eyes. Then opened them. Sleep wouldn't come. She reached for the Bible and opened it up to the book of Psalms, reading over the first few chapters, not sure what she was looking for.

A verse in chapter three jumped out at her. *I lay down and slept; I woke again, for the LORD sustained me.*

"You're the One who sustains me, aren't You, God?" she whispered into the still air. The idea of releasing her worries to God and trusting Him to protect her was appealing and freeing.

What about trusting God with her future?

McKenna shifted, wrestling in her mind with the words and not coming up with an answer. "Help me trust You, God," she whispered.

The quiet sounds of the night calmed her, helped her relax into the blanket. She would have said sleep would be impossible after the day they'd had, but she felt exhaustion and peace washing over her.

She fell asleep watching the northern lights.

THIRTEEN

McKenna could tell when she blinked her eyes open that the light outside was too bright for it to be her turn for a shift. As she'd suspected he would, Will had taken both shifts, staying awake all night so she could rest.

She stretched her arms and sat up, gathering and folding the wool blanket she'd put between herself and the tundra grass while she slept. Despite the uneven ground, it was the best night of sleep she'd had in recent memory.

"Good morning." Will's smile warmed her all the way through. "Did you sleep well?"

"Wonderfully, thank you."

"Good." He handed her a blue metal camp mug full of dark brown liquid.

Her eyebrows rose. "Is this…?"

"Coffee?" He laughed. "Yes. Dug it and the stuff to make it over the campfire out of my emergency kit."

"Those are my kind of emergency preparations right there," she said before taking a long sip of the dark brew. She closed her eyes and sighed. "That is delicious."

"Coffee over a fire is the best kind."

"You think of everything, did you know that?" She took another sip.

"Listen, McKenna. About last night…"

"Yeah?"

He set his coffee mug down and met her eyes. It was part of what she loved about him, she realized. His ability to look straight in her eyes and never back down, no matter how stubborn she got. Her mom had told her when she was a teenager that she was going to have to find a strong man to be in a relationship with, that she'd walk all over someone who was mild mannered.

Will Harrison was strong.

And at the moment thoroughly capable of breaking her heart. She swallowed hard and forced her gaze to hold steady. "What is it?"

"I don't know. I, uh, I don't know if I need to apologize to you for kissing you…"

Her heart sank straight to her toes.

"Or apologize for taking so long to do it."

McKenna opened her mouth to reply, but the whir of a small-plane engine overhead drew their attention to the sky.

"Some time for a rescue."

Will raised his eyebrows and grinned at her and McKenna felt herself blushing at the words she'd had no intention of saying out loud.

"Look at that. Loosening up a little, after all, aren't you?"

She shoved him.

They watched as Rick's plane landed and he climbed out. "I got worried when you didn't show at the office," he explained to Will. "You're always good about calling when you're not coming in and you didn't this time." He looked at the wreckage. "Now I know why."

Rick turned back to them. "Is everything okay?" he asked with concern. "I saw you push this guy." He looked at McKenna and motioned toward Will. "Is he bothering you? What happened anyway? Why were you guys out here? I'm guessing it's not a hunting trip...?"

McKenna wasn't sure if he meant to imply anything or not, but his endless questions and possible insinuations made her bristle. "The plane crashed," she said instead, not wanting to answer any questions but curious as to whether his reaction to their crash would tell her anything about his validity as a suspect.

"*That* I guessed on my own." He gestured to the wreckage and then turned to Will. "Mechanical failure or pilot error?"

While she wanted to see his reaction, she didn't necessarily want the plane's sabotage to be common knowledge. She tensed as she waited for Will to answer.

"Mechanical failure, it looks like."

Rick nodded. "Glad it wasn't your fault. And that you two are okay. How about a ride back to Barrow?"

Will looked to her. She felt her confidence in her abilities as a trooper grow at the fact that he'd waited to see what she wanted to do. He was letting her handle it.

McKenna debated their options. They needed to leave, and she didn't think either of them should leave without the other. On the other hand, if they had any hope of getting a crime scene team to help them figure out what happened, it would be better to leave someone at the plane to ensure nothing was tampered with.

But what if she or Will stayed and something happened to them?

"A ride back would be good." The likelihood that someone could obliterate a crime scene this large was minimal. She'd call Captain Wilkins, see if he could get in touch with someone in Anchorage and get a team up here as soon as possible.

"Let's go, then. You're lucky I was in the area."

"Scouting out places to take clients?" Will asked.

Rick nodded as he readied the plane for takeoff. McKenna felt herself stiffen at the idea of flying again, after falling out of the sky in a worthless piece of metal that had once been a plane. It was good that they had to get back to town so she could conquer this new fear immediately. Otherwise, given the choice, she'd probably never fly again.

"Yeah."

"It's too close to the coast for most of the game we hunt," Will noted. "Caribou tend to stay farther south."

Rick nodded again. "Yeah, that's what I noticed, too."

McKenna frowned. Hadn't Rick been a hunting guide in this area for longer than Will? Shouldn't he already know this wasn't a prime hunting spot for his clients?

Only polar bears really made this part of the land their home. And as McKenna had seen for herself the day before, there were fewer of them populating the area than ever. Someone was killing them, endangering not only their species but the balance of the wilderness food chain.

She might not be the best at solving puzzles and things like double murders, but now that this case was clearly wildlife related, she knew she'd get whoever was behind it eventually.

Could the killer be Rick? And if so, had he come out to save them…or to take them out for good?

"She's ready when you guys are," Rick called over the noise of the airplane.

Will glanced down at his SAT phone, deciding that since they were going to be home within hours it was safe to use. He'd better fulfill his promise to McKenna and let her call Captain Wilkins as soon as possible.

Giving Rick the "one minute" sign, he held the phone toward her. "Did you want to call Wilkins?"

She nodded, reaching for the phone and then stopping. "I don't have his number." Her face paled. "I can't believe I don't have his number!"

"Hey—" he laid a hand on her arm "—don't panic. I've got another idea."

McKenna's face was still colorless as Will dialed a number on the phone that he knew by heart.

"Hello?"

"Luke, it's Will."

"Hey! I didn't recognize the number. Wait, is this your SAT number?" Knowing that Will would only use the SAT phone in an emergency, Luke's voice immediately transitioned from friend to law enforcement officer.

For a second, Will questioned his decision to ask Luke to contact McKenna's boss for them. He was, first and foremost, her big brother. Hearing about the crash would awaken all his protective instincts.

Which is what the alarmed look on McKenna's face said, too, as she shook her head.

"Yeah. My plane crashed yesterday. No injuries, thankfully. But I need you to do me a favor."

"Go ahead."

"McKenna's with me. Can you call her boss, Captain Wilkins? He needs to know that this happened so he can send out a crime scene team. I think someone might have tampered with the plane. We're east of Barrow, not too far from the coast. I have coordinates for you."

"Let me get a pen. Okay, go ahead."

Will recited the numbers.

"Got it. I'll call him. You think using a SAT phone is going to enable anyone to find you who shouldn't?"

"Already thought of it. That's why we waited it out yesterday, to see if someone from town would find us before we'd need to use the phone. We were found this morning."

"So you're leaving now." Luke sounded relieved, and then his tone changed again. "You spent all night with my sister?"

"While she slept and I watched the fire. You know me better than that."

"Okay. Call me when you get to Barrow. Who found you?"

"My boss."

"Have McKenna call me when she's home."

"I will."

"Do the best you can to keep her safe."

"I will."

He ended the call and looked up to meet McKenna's glare. "You called my *brother* of all people?"

He shrugged. "Yeah, he's worried. He wants you to call him as soon as you get home. But he was the best choice to rely on to get word to Captain Wilkins."

"I guess you're right," she admitted grudgingly.

"As usual." He teased.

"Ha." A flicker of a grin teased the corners of her mouth. "You're right *this* time. But there's a first time for everything."

"Are we leaving or what?" Rick yelled from the plane. Will thought he saw a flash of annoyance on his boss's face. He'd only kept Rick waiting for a few minutes, but it had probably been a stressful morning for him, wondering about Will's whereabouts. Maybe he should cut Rick some slack.

"We'd better get in," he told McKenna, climbing into the plane behind her.

He noticed she squeezed her eyes shut as she buckled the seat belt and then took slow, deep breaths as Rick eased the plane into the air.

He grabbed her hand. "You okay?"

She nodded, not opening her eyes. "Mostly."

"Not excited about flying again?"

"No." Her clipped tone said all it needed to.

He squeezed her hand tighter and she squeezed back. It was all the confirmation he needed not to let go, even when Rick caught his eye and raised his eyebrows.

Okay, yes, so he could see what his boss was probably thinking. Maybe the local wildlife trooper and a hunting guide weren't the most logical match. But he and McKenna had been dancing on the edge of something more than friends for long enough. When this case finally slowed down, he'd finish the talk he'd meant to have with her that morning, let her know that this time he wasn't going anywhere.

He still questioned whether he should have left Seward in the first place, the first time their relationship might have been blossoming into something more. But he needed to stop worrying over the past. He'd loved Rachael and believed God had put them together on purpose, even if their time was short.

But he also believed God was putting him and McKenna together now.

He just needed to keep her safe long enough to tell her.

Will studied her face, the frown lines that were faintly etched across her pretty features. He wished he could make this whole mess go away.

"Who'd you have to call?" Rick tossed the words over his shoulder, not taking his eyes off the front window.

"My brother," McKenna answered for him. "He's a bit overprotective."

"Ah."

Rick didn't comment further, and McKenna didn't, either. Will noticed she'd left out the message they'd passed on to her boss, and the fact that Luke was a police officer.

Because she suspected Rick more than she had earlier, or because she wanted to limit the people who knew all that information?

He didn't know. This case had so many aspects he felt unsure about.

That uncertainty carried over to his private life, too—and his ever-growing feelings for the woman beside him. She'd kissed him back, but had it been more the emotion of their situation and less about her wanting to take their relationship beyond friendship?

At the moment, he couldn't decide which possibility worried him more.

McKenna woke later that night to Mollie's tongue on her arm, licking and nudging her over and over.

She squeezed her eyes shut tighter and tried to pull her arm away. "Go back to sleep, Mollie," she mumbled, hoping the dog would lie back down and let her catch a few more hours before she dived headfirst back into work.

Mollie ignored her, her nudges becoming more insistent till her pointy German shepherd nose was all but punching McKenna in the arm. McKenna sat up in bed, trying to coax herself to get up and let the dog out to use the bathroom, or howl at the moon, or whatever she was planning.

She shuffled to the door, wishing she had a flashlight to keep herself from stepping on anything she'd left on the floor.

McKenna squinted down at her feet. She could see better than she normally could at this time of night. A peek through the blinds told her it wasn't a full moon.

She looked around the room again, suddenly realizing that something wasn't right. Was someone in the house?

McKenna leaned forward, just enough to see out the open bedroom door and into the hallway. A faint orange glow pulsed from somewhere in the common area. Alarm bells exploded in her mind just as her nose identified the smell of smoke.

The house was on fire.

"Mollie, come!"

The dog darted toward her and McKenna gave her a quick scratch behind the ears in gratitude for saving both of their lives. The smoke detectors had never gone off, and she was sure that further investigation would reveal that they'd had the batteries taken out. McKenna hurried into the living room, where flames were just starting to lick up the far walls. It looked as if the blaze had started at the opposite end of the house from the guest room where she slept—maybe in Matt's office. She tried to memorize as many details about the scene as she could, in case it could help with the investigation she knew would be coming. Then she grabbed the backpack with her case file that she'd left at the foot of the couch last night after looking over her notes from the day.

McKenna eased the back door open slowly, not wanting to add oxygen to the fire—and definitely not wanting to draw any attention if the killer-turned-arsonist was waiting for her outside.

The small backyard area and the street behind the Dixons' house both looked clear.

Satisfied that it was as safe outside as it could be, McKenna motioned to Mollie, and the two of them moved away from the house, watching the fire do its work from the outside as she called the fire department on her cell phone. After hanging up with them, she texted Will.

And then there was nothing she could do but wait and watch the merciless flames destroy the house of people who had been so generous with her. The fire department showed up quickly and worked to put out the fire, but most of the house had been destroyed by then. McKenna brushed an unexpected tear from her eye, wrestling with emotions she couldn't explain. As the blaze was brought under control by the men and women working, a heat inside her began to build. It was the same indignation she'd felt after Anna had been shot. This was out of control. The killer had to be stopped because clearly he was getting more and more desperate to hurt her. Did he really want her dead that badly?

Her shoulders shook with silent, tearless sobs. She wished she had tears to go with them, but they wouldn't come.

A soft hand on her shoulder startled her, comforted her and made her feel self-conscious simultaneously.

"You'll find him," was all Will said. No empty promises that things would be okay. No awkward words of comfort. This man who knew her so well said the only thing he could say that would encourage her to keep going.

McKenna sniffed. "I can only hope so. I never should have let you talk me into staying here." McKenna swiped a hand across her cheek, brushing another stray tear away.

"I thought it would be best."

McKenna looked back toward the charred remains of the Dixons' house, then had to tear her gaze away. She felt sick as she realized that, once again, her choice to stay here had caused this.

Will felt sick. He knew how hard Matt had worked to fix that house up just the way his wife had wanted it.

"Best?" McKenna turned from studying the scene and leveled him with a glare. "You call two people losing their home and everything they have, when their lives have already been turned upside down because someone shot Anna, *best?* Would you please let me handle this from now on? I don't want anyone else to get hurt because they're trying to help me. I'm in charge here, I need to be the one making the decisions and carrying the responsibility. As I've tried to tell you more than once, I can handle everything *just fine*."

Her words so echoed Rachael's the night before she'd been killed that it felt almost as if she'd slapped him in the face and sent him back in time.

"It's dangerous," he'd told Rachael when she'd informed him of her skiing plans.

She'd only laughed.

"I mean it, Rachael. Be careful." He'd considered his options, realized he wasn't going to talk her out of it and then changed his tactics. "At least let me come with you. I know the wilderness—I can read signs that might point to animal danger or avalanches. Let me help."

"I don't need help, Will. I'm perfectly capable and can handle a ski trip just fine on my own. But thanks for the offer."

She'd left the next morning and he'd never seen her alive again.

He jerked out of his memory back into the present, the smell of smoke highlighting the danger this stubborn woman in front of him was trying to ignore.

"Just let me help."

"No!"

The past and present tangled as his frustration rose. "You're being unreasonable, Rachael!"

He realized his mistake milliseconds before hurt flashed in McKenna's eyes.

"McKenna..." Will reached for her arm.

"No, Will. I'm not her." She swallowed hard and for a moment he thought she might cry. She didn't. "And I don't need your help."

This time it was his turn to take a step back. He wanted to protect her, to help her end this case safely.

But it seemed she'd made her choice. Independent McKenna didn't need anyone. He should have known all along this was what she wanted—to be left alone.

He walked straight to his truck, climbed in and drove away without looking back, heading out of town toward the wilderness. Maybe he'd sit by one of the lakes outside town for a little while. The space might give him the room he needed to think.

All this time, he'd wanted to help and protect her, just as he had when she was a kid. But that urge to look out for her, to fix things for her, had backfired, driving her away.

McKenna didn't need him. And now, it seemed, she didn't even want him around.

He'd been foolish to think she did. When he'd run into her, literally, at the grocery store, he'd noticed she was all grown up. He would have had to be blind not to. And this new woman version of McKenna he had gotten to know was the woman he was falling for, had probably already fallen for. Maybe he was guilty of being a little overprotective. But was it so wrong to want to protect the woman he cared so much about?

He pulled up beside one of the lakes, opened the door of his truck and listened to the quiet, the peacefulness of the arctic air contrasting with the churning in his gut from the events of that night.

There in the darkness, understanding about where he'd messed up finally hit him. Different as the two women were, different as his *feelings* for them were, he'd treated the situation as if it was Rachael all over again. His slip earlier—calling McKenna by Rachael's name—had proven that, his heart admitting it subconsciously before his mind was able to.

"Why, God?" he let himself ask aloud. "What's so wrong with trying to be a protector?"

Scenes of his life flashed through his mind. Choices he'd made. Choices Rachael had made. He'd always wanted to take care of his wife, give her everything she could ever want and treat her like a princess. That hadn't been what Rachael had had in mind—she'd wanted to take care of herself, to choose her own adventures without his interference and his need to keep her safe. Maybe they hadn't been a perfectly compatible match. But that hadn't meant he'd loved her any less. Will wished she'd lived, wished he'd been able to do more to convince her not to ski that day.

But she'd made her own choices.

"Is that it, God?"

Pieces of a long-undone puzzle fell together in Will's mind. He'd given McKenna a hard time about her lack of trust in God, her desire to be in control, yet didn't he struggle with the same thing? Maybe his struggle looked a little different. But he was guilty at times of wanting to *over*protect.

But Will wasn't God. And in the end, people made choices and only God could watch over them. Will couldn't always be enough. Not for Rachael. McKenna had been right. Her death hadn't been his fault.

He couldn't be enough for McKenna, either.

But with God's help, Will would do the best he could. If McKenna would let him.

He pulled his phone from his pocket and glanced at it, knowing he needed to give her some space but wishing she'd call. Text. Something.

Will might have finally made peace with his past, decided he was ready to move on. But that didn't mean McKenna would welcome him back into her life.

* * *

"I have news. Did you want to wait for Will to come back?" the man from the fire department asked McKenna.

She shrugged. *Was* Will coming back? As much as she'd been hurt by his slip—calling her Rachael, reminding her once again that Will had been in love before, with a woman she could never measure up to—she hadn't expected that her words would drive him away. But somehow she'd seen the hurt she felt mirrored in his eyes when she'd refused his help and told him to leave her alone. She sensed that he wasn't coming back anytime soon. Maybe not ever. "You'd better just go ahead and tell me," she decided.

"Are you ready?" the man asked carefully, looking as if he was preparing to gauge her reaction.

McKenna sighed. "Sure."

"It's arson. No doubt about it. The burn pattern indicates it clearly already. There will be more of an investigation. The guys from the police department will probably be out to help and we'll need to send samples off to the lab to confirm our preliminary ruling and see what kind of accelerant was used. But yeah, someone wanted to burn this house down." He shook his head. "Any idea why?"

None she was willing to share. McKenna shrugged again and the firefighter walked away. She stood and surveyed the damage for herself, then walked closer to the house, which was now a stark contrast between piles of ash and broken glass and parts of the house looking the way they always had. Matt's study had definitely gotten the worst of it. She'd be willing to bet that's where the fire had started.

"Excuse me." She motioned over the man who had spoken to her. "Can you tell me where it started?"

"Officially we can't say yet."

"But...?"

He weighed his words. "I'd guess it started right there." He gestured toward the study.

"Thank you." McKenna couldn't have been less surprised. Whoever was here hadn't only been trying to kill her, although she was sure that would have been a bonus. They'd also been trying to destroy her notes on this case and the evidence she'd gathered, likely guessing she'd been using the study as an at-home office.

It was a good thing she'd forgotten to put that backpack away last night.

He also must have known she was taking her notes back to the house where she was staying, because otherwise the trooper post, not the house, would have been the target.

It couldn't have been ten whole seconds from when she had that thought to when half the firefighters suddenly packed up and jumped back onto their trucks, clearly preparing to face another fire.

Goose bumps crawled down her arms and she motioned for Mollie to stay while she ran toward one of the trucks that was leaving. "Excuse me," she began, praying her gut feeling was wrong this time. "Where are you headed?"

The man blinked, looking surprised to see her. "Aren't you the new wildlife trooper?"

She nodded.

"I figured you'd called it in. We're headed to another fire. This one at the trooper post."

McKenna motioned for Mollie and jumped into her own car, following them to another fire that looked eerily like the first.

"It's burning just like the house did," she heard one of the men shout as they struggled to extinguish the blaze. Most likely the same accelerant had been used—further proof that the two fires had been set by the same person.

She watched the already exhausted men give everything

they had to get the fire under control. But this time the fire was too strong, too fast, for the little building.

In a matter of minutes, the entire structure was gone. McKenna tried to blink away the shock but couldn't process the scene before her. She was so deep into this case, felt as if she was so close to solving it, and now this. Her office was destroyed—all the files stored in the office were gone. Most of those had only existed as hard copies, since her predecessor hadn't believed in digitizing his office. The notes in her backpack were all she had left.

She hoped that would be enough.

FOURTEEN

"Hello?" Will picked up the landline the next morning, rubbing his eyes, which were dry from lack of sleep, before he glanced at the caller ID and saw the call was coming from Truman Hunting Expeditions.

"You coming in to work today?" Rick's voice sounded more harried than usual.

"I'd planned to take the day off. I don't have any hunts scheduled." Will glanced at the clock. Just past six.

"Change those plans. I've got a group in from Washington that wants to go out today."

"We should have left already to get good time in."

"Am I the boss here, or are you?"

Will let several seconds of silence tick by before he sighed. He may as well work today. It wasn't as if he was going to do anyone any good sticking around town. "I'll be there in thirty minutes," he said and hung up.

Will picked up his cell phone out of habit. No missed calls or texts, which was a good sign. McKenna must have had a quiet night after the fire was taken care of.

Of course, she might not be letting him know those things anymore. After all, *she* was in charge of this investigation and could handle it herself.

The words she'd thrown at him yesterday still burned,

despite the revelations he'd had last night. He was sorry he'd called her Rachael. But if she'd only been in his head, she'd understand why the situations had seemed so similar, why the wrong name had slipped even though he knew full well which woman he was with.

He'd originally taken today off work to help McKenna. But he doubted she'd welcome his help after yesterday.

Actually, he was sure of it. She'd made it clear she didn't need him.

He'd probably be better off if he could get used to that idea. And in the process somehow convince his heart he didn't need her either.

He was still staring at the phone when it rang, showing Matt's number. He answered immediately. "Hey, what's up? Everything all right with Anna?"

"Yeah, she's doing great. That's why I'm calling. We've decided Lexi's going to stay here with her and I'm coming back to Barrow."

"You're sure that's a good idea?" Since no further attempts had been made on Anna's life while she'd been hospitalized, he was less worried about her than he'd been initially, but it had still made sense for Matt to stay with his sister-in-law, offer some level of protection.

"Lexi insists. And you know her—she can handle anything. She just lets me pretend to be the protector." He laughed.

Will knew his friend was probably right. His own heart clenched as he thought about the similarities in Lexi and McKenna's personalities. He knew, somewhere deep in his heart, that McKenna was capable. Would it hurt for her to humor him and let him feel as if he was helping her somehow?

Or maybe he was being overly protective. Behaving more like a brother than a man who was in love with her, treating her like a child instead of acknowledging her as a smart, competent woman. After all, her fiercely independent streak was one of the reasons she'd stolen his heart in the first place.

He shrugged away the thoughts of McKenna. He'd had enough introspection for the day. "I'll be glad when you're back. It's not the same here without you to talk to after work."

"My flight lands late this afternoon. Think you can pick me up at the airport?"

"Yeah. But we need to talk about your house."

"McKenna already called last night and told Lexi about the fire."

"You're okay?"

"It's just a house. Seeing Anna hurt like she was really put things in perspective. We'll build another one. For now, just pick me up at the airport and let me know what I can do to help with the case."

"You're not exactly the top pick on the troopers' list of people to confide in." He laughed as he said the words, knowing Matt was able to handle a little ribbing.

"That life feels like a thousand years ago. Besides, you wouldn't believe some of the people I know and things I've learned from them. Maybe I can figure out how this guy thinks, help you and McKenna catch him somehow."

"Yeah, we should talk about McKenna, too."

"The fact that you're in love with her? Figured that out about two weeks ago."

"About the fact that she's not talking to me after I said the wrong thing last night."

"Double murders, woman troubles… You do have a mess on your hands. Just lay low for today. Give her some space. I'll do whatever I can to help you get her back, man. I haven't seen you so…*alive* since you got to Barrow."

Will knew he was right. The truth was that he *hadn't* felt so alive since he moved here. "Lay low?" He felt uneasy at the idea of leaving her alone when someone was after her, but hadn't she asked for that? If him showing up to talk to her would make her angry or distracted then it could put her off her game at a time when she badly needed to stay focused.

"Look, you don't sound as if you like the idea. Maybe I'm the wrong person to talk to. What would Luke tell you to do?"

"Lay low."

"Maybe it's not a bad idea then."

Will knew it wasn't. He'd take his friend's advice and leave her alone, at least for today. Although he'd probably drive by her office later, just to make sure she was there and everything seemed normal. Sometime tomorrow, he'd be on her doorstep, ready to plead his case. Because he wasn't letting her go without at least trying.

He wasn't two hours into his day at work when Will finally admitted to himself that putting McKenna out of his thoughts—even for a day—was never going to work.

Everything about her was ingrained in his life. Her laugh. The way the sun glinted off her shiny red hair. The stubborn lift of her chin.

He'd give anything to pawn off this latest batch of clients to someone else and get back to her. She was invading his mind even more than usual and he couldn't shake the feeling he'd made the wrong choice going in to work today.

"How many caribou do you think we'll get today?" one of the clients asked from behind him.

"It depends," Will answered without taking his eyes from the plane's dash. Rick had loaned him a plane since

Will's had been unfixable and he hadn't gotten insurance money to replace it yet.

"You like the taste of 'em?" another man asked the first.

He laughed. "Nah. Just need another trophy for my wall."

Will bristled. McKenna was right about men like these. The local wildlife *needed* protection from them.

He hated to tell her about days like this, though, because it reflected badly on hunters in general. And plenty of men, himself and Matt included, liked to hunt and did so responsibly.

Unfortunately the clients at Truman Hunting Expeditions who respected the wildlife and the land were few and far between these days. The situation had only been getting worse in the past couple of months.

Will was beginning to think the business was in trouble. Rick used to have higher standards for screening clients, always making sure they were capable and had received some instruction before heading out on a hunting trip. He'd also heard Rick on the phone recently talking about money in a low, tense voice. Maybe that was what was driving him to be less choosy about the clients he signed up for packages.

Not that it was really any of Will's business.

"Wait while I get us set up," he instructed the men, eyeing one of them who seemed to be having a little trouble with his muzzle control. When he'd exited the plane, he'd been a little too relaxed in his handling of the rifle. And as he talked to one of the other guys in the group, he'd swept the front of the gun across several people. Will had cringed at the violation of basic gun safety—never point a gun at anything you don't mean to shoot, and treat every gun as if it was loaded.

Thankfully, that one wasn't. Yet. Will rubbed at his temples, feeling a headache coming on. This was going to be a long day. He glanced up at the herd of caribou in the distance. Not close enough yet, but maybe in a few minutes.

He laid his pack across the ground as a rifle rest and waited.

"I see them right there!" one of the men exclaimed, gesturing with the business end of his rifle.

"Keep that pointed at the ground until we're ready to shoot," Will directed him. The man scowled but did as instructed.

He really needed to start his business. And soon. Maybe sooner than he'd thought.

Will watched the herd for another minute. Several of the caribou wandered close enough that they might have had a shot, but they were turned the wrong way, facing away from them. While it might be possible to get one at this range, a clean shot through the heart wasn't likely, and nothing else would be a humane kill.

"I'm beginning to think you didn't bring us out here to get anything, after all," one of the men said in an angry tone.

"I'm gonna get one anyway," his friend announced, kneeling down to use the rest Will had set up.

"Not yet. We don't have a good shot."

The man loaded and chambered the rifle. Will told him again to take the gun out of shooting position and wait, but he didn't listen, so Will used his foot to nudge the rest away so the man had nothing to balance his rifle on.

"What do you think you're doing?" he growled at Will. "Fine." He stood and before Will could react, he aimed his rifle and took a cheap shot. Will cringed, knowing what that shot would do to an animal if it hit. It was an inhumane shot, that was all there was to it. Fortunately, the man had terrible aim and didn't manage to hit anything at all.

Will watched as the caribou herd started to run, startled by the clap of gunfire.

"None of you has a good enough shot. Put the guns down or I will get in that plane and leave all three of you for the bears."

"We have guns."

"Loaded with a round that may or may not be heavy enough to stop a grizzly." Will shrugged and turned to the plane. "Your choice."

In his peripheral vision, he saw them look at one another and then reluctantly lower their weapons.

"We'll shoot when we have a good opportunity. A humane one," Will said, his voice firm. No wonder McKenna viewed some hunters the way she did. The way this group had been acting, he didn't feel like any of them deserved a chance to bag a caribou today. But for the sake of his job, he'd give it one more try. Then he could legitimately call their day over, to give them enough time to get back to Barrow.

Three hours later, Will drove away from Truman Hunting Expeditions, his pesky cargo finally no longer his responsibility. He let out a deep breath, trying to calm the pounding of his heart. It could have been a lot worse. At least no one had gotten hurt with the sloppy way they'd handled those guns. Any of them could easily have killed one of their hunting partners.

The scene on the tundra that McKenna had described popped into his mind. Two dead. He'd have to ask her if it was possible that it could have been a hunting trip gone wrong, maybe not murder, after all.

Though that didn't explain why someone was after McKenna for investigating it.

Will let out a deep breath, the stress of both the case and the day pressing on him with a weight almost too heavy to handle. He couldn't take any more of this. He was close enough to the amount in savings he'd wanted to have before he started his business. Will would call Rick as soon as he got home and ask for a meeting, maybe even for the next day.

He couldn't leave this company soon enough.

McKenna hadn't expected to sleep, being back in the house where Anna had been shot, but exhaustion had overcome her and she'd slept all the way through the night.

She'd called Lexi the night before to let her know about the fire. Lexi hadn't seemed as concerned about the house as she had been about McKenna's safety. She could hear Matt in the background, sounding as if he felt the same way.

McKenna hadn't known what to say or do, other than to apologize profusely for her part in their house's destruction, and to try to reassure them she'd be as careful as she could. They'd told her that Anna was improving and should be out of the hospital within a week.

That gave her a week to get this case wrapped up. There was no way her friend needed to come back to a town where the person who had tried to kill her was still at large. As McKenna drained a cup of strong coffee and looked out into the clear fall day, she didn't feel as if she'd need a week. She had almost everything she needed.

McKenna pulled out the notes she'd been taking on the case, lingering for a long time on the ones she'd taken after she and Will talked about the profile of a hunter.

She frowned.

Flipped back a couple of pages in the notebook, to the night Anna had brought her to the murder scene on the beach—Seth Davison.

She'd jotted down descriptions of everything she'd seen.

Even the fact that the camo pants and jacket Seth was wearing had looked brand-new. McKenna flipped back to the notes from her conversation with Will, reliving what he'd said again in her mind. Would an experienced hunter wear brand-new gear on a hunt? Maybe....

But something else struck her. Only his wallet and a cell phone had been recovered from the scene of the crime, and when she'd checked with the hotel he'd been checked into, the room where he'd stayed was empty.

If he was in town to hunt...where was his rifle?

What if he hadn't been there to hunt at all?

The thought morphed from a tickle in the back of her mind, to a clear thought, to a solid suspicion. Seth Davison hadn't been in Barrow to hunt. He'd been in Barrow to investigate the deaths of his friends.

If that was true—*if*—it told her several things. First, he'd thought the hunting industry had been connected to the deaths somehow, a hunch that may or may not be true. Second, he'd believed his friends' deaths to be the result of foul play. Third, he didn't trust anyone else to investigate the murders. It was a lot of trouble to fly up and investigate on his own, especially if McKenna's hunch was correct and Seth wasn't a hunter himself.

McKenna almost had it. She was sure of it. She just needed to think through everything and connect the dots. A shiver of anticipation went up her arms as she realized that this really could be the day this nightmare ended.

She jotted down her thoughts in the notebook, then flipped it back to the first page. She rose from her seat, put her used coffee mug in the sink, motioned to Mollie to stay and headed outside to her vehicle with a copy of her case notes. At the last minute, she decided she didn't want to have the notes on her, just in case whoever had been following her chose today to try to take them from her. No, she'd just take a fresh notebook and a pen, and work from memory and from the notes she hoped to collect today from Chris. Instead, she put the notes back inside the house, shoving them inside a cereal box in the pantry in case anyone decided to break in and search for them.

Her thoughts ventured back to Chris. He'd seemed surprised when she'd called last night to ask to talk to him. Of course, it had been late. Or was he surprised because he'd set the fire and expected her to be dead?

Too much had happened to her and to those around her in the past week or so. McKenna could hardly separate her worthwhile thoughts from paranoia.

She drove to Bear's Tooth Pub and Pizzeria, where they'd agreed to meet, and hoped the churning in her stomach wasn't some kind of survival instinct telling her to ditch this meeting and hole up somewhere safe. It better not be; she couldn't afford to do that. One way or another, this had to end.

And maybe talking to Chris was the key.

She exited the car, careful to lock it behind her. She'd parked in a location where she could keep an eye on it from inside the pizza place, so she thankfully wouldn't have to worry about the possibility of anyone tampering with it.

Chris was already waiting for her. And he'd taken her seat.

Every trooper, police officer and law enforcement worker she'd ever known always chose the same seat. Back to the wall, facing the door. Chris had picked the right booth, but he was on the wrong side.

"Any chance you'd want to switch seats?" She forced herself to keep the question casual, her tone light.

"Law enforcement. I forgot." He shrugged and switched sides, surprising her with his willingness to accommodate her. "What did you want to talk about?"

"Those bodies we found on the tundra that first day I was in town."

Had he flinched, or had she imagined it?

Chris leaned back in his chair. "Getting right to it, I guess. No pizza first? No, I guess this isn't really a pizza kind of conversation."

"You're not answering my question."

"Look, I've been doing this a long time. I've never seen anything like that and no, I wasn't responsible. Are we done here?"

"No, we're not."

"I have questions, too, as long as we're asking. Like, why would you have a hunting guide serve as your pilot? Isn't that a conflict of interest? Especially when another pilot is available."

Would he be questioning her, implying that maybe *she* had something to do with the murders if he was guilty? It was either a brilliant ploy to throw her off, or he really did suspect her. Which would make him innocent.

She wanted to say it was none of his business, but that would end this conversation, leaving her no better off than before she'd come in.

"I've known Will all my life. We grew up together. After showing up new in town, and getting thrown right into a murder investigation, I felt more comfortable working with someone familiar. I'm sorry you're offended that I've been using another pilot."

He shrugged. McKenna decided to try again to see if she could startle him into giving away any useful information.

"I'm being followed." She decided she might as well go for broke. "I've felt it for weeks. But it's funny, I didn't feel like anyone was following me on my way here. Any idea why that is?" She locked her gaze with his. He said nothing.

Suspicion crawled up her arms. "No comment?"

"Look. I don't have to explain myself to you. Anything I've done has been legal and fully justified." He shoved his chair back. "We're done here. Somehow I thought you might have decided you needed my help, but it's clear that's not the case." He reached for his back pocket and McKenna jerked, hand hovering near her weapon.

He glared at her as he slowly pulled out a wallet and grabbed a five. "Calm down, Trooper Clark. Just thought I'd pay my bill. Like the law-abiding citizen I am, despite what you think." He snatched the bill sitting on the table from the cola he'd been drinking and slammed it and the money on the front counter on his way out.

McKenna watched him pull out of the parking lot, keeping an eye on her car as well, as she thought through their conversation. He was evasive, that was for sure. But while it had seemed as if he was intentionally leaving her in the dark on some things, making her think that he might be the person who had been following her, his answers had convinced her that he was innocent of the murders. If she was right, that left Rick or George.

It was time to talk to both of the other men. One way or the other, if she was right, she'd soon be face-to-face with a killer.

FIFTEEN

McKenna had tried all day to resist the urge to call Will. There were so many good reasons not to, the first being the fact that she wasn't sure how much longer she could continue trying to have a casual friendship with a man who made her stomach do backflips every time he came near her.

She'd known in high school that Will Harrison was a special kind of guy. What she hadn't known was that her feelings for him wouldn't weaken over the years. But she was old enough now to know better than to get invested in the wrong guy. Wasn't she? They weren't suited for each other. First, he still seemed to think of her as Luke's little sister, in need of protection from the dangerous world. Second, their personalities were so opposite. Will didn't understand her need for structure. He called it control.

Control wasn't bad. There was something to be said for having a plan.

And sometimes there was something to be said for taking a chance. Besides, she had developments in the case she wanted to discuss with him. She dialed his number.

Will's phone rang a few times and then went to voice mail. "Will, it's me." McKenna hesitated, not sure how much she should say on a message. "Never mind. I'm going to try to call you again," she said and then hung up and hit Redial.

Still no answer.

She tried again and got voice mail again. She sighed, deciding she'd rather leave him with at least some idea of why she'd called, in case he couldn't get in touch with her right away. "It's McKenna again. I'm sorry for yesterday, when I said I'd be fine on my own. The truth is, I like having you to bounce ideas off of. Forgive me? I figured some things out about the case…" She let her voice trail off as she approached a crossroads. "I'd rather talk about them in person, but you should know that I'm going to check out two more leads and if for some reason you need them, I've left a copy of my case notes in a box of Cheerios in my pantry." She laughed at herself. "Yeah, I know, kind of random. But it was the best hiding place I could think of."

Movement out of the driver's-side window caught her eye, but not soon enough for it to do her any good. A car barreled toward her much faster than the speed limit allowed. McKenna winced, closing her eyes and stomping on the brakes simultaneously in the hopes of avoiding a collision or at least lessening the impact.

The crunch of metal on metal assaulted her ears as the seat belt caught her and bit into her skin. She gasped from the impact, which threw her into the door and then back.

She stayed still, almost holding her breath, not sure if it was because she was stunned or because she was trying to make sure she was okay. McKenna had no idea how much time passed as she sat there, hands still on the wheel with the deflated air bag between them. She only knew that she sat in the passenger seat blinking for what felt like an eternity.

Eventually she remembered the phone in her hand. Will wasn't going to be thrilled when he got this voice mail.

"Sorry. I got in a little wreck. I think the guy might be drunk, because there's no way he couldn't have seen me." She remained in her seat, waiting for the other driver to approach her.

But the person who stepped out of the other car was clad from head to toe in black. Complete with a ski mask.

It hadn't been a drunk driver. Which could only mean the crash was deliberate.

Air whooshed out of her lungs as McKenna realized the man's intent. "Not a drunk. He's coming closer—this is about to be an abduction. He's tall. Broad shoulders. Will, help me. Get those papers."

The man jerked the door open and McKenna hung up the phone, shoving it in her pocket and praying it wouldn't be found.

"Nice try," a gravelly voice said with derision.

She tried to play dumb. "What?"

"You get it out, or I'll get it for you. Understand?"

McKenna shivered. Slowly, she pulled the phone from her pocket, feeling as if she had no other choice, but at the same time as if she'd given away her only lifeline. She tried to think back to trooper academy. Was there any kind of training that would tell her what she was supposed to do in this situation? Nothing came to mind in the heat of the moment.

What would Luke tell her to do?

That was easy. Luke would have told her not to get into this mess in the first place. As though she'd had a choice.

Rough hands grabbed McKenna by the shoulders, hauled her out of the car and shoved her into the car that had hit her, all in one motion. The streets were oddly empty, not a single witness as far as she could tell. Her stomach churned and she felt her palms start to sweat.

She'd woken up this morning determined that this would

be the day this case came to an end. And maybe it would be. But certainly not according to how she'd planned.

Will had asked Rick for a meeting, with plans to tell him he was quitting, and the other man had agreed. But it was past the time they'd set and Will hadn't seen or heard from him.

He glanced down at the clock on his phone. Rick was twenty minutes late.

He'd always been a punctual guy. This wasn't like him. Although he had been changing in the past few months.

Will glanced at his phone, noting the time. He hated to bother Rick's desk again, guilt had gnawed at him after the last time he'd seen his calendar. But this was a dangerous place and they were in a dangerous business. He needed to check Rick's schedule and see if he could figure out what might have delayed him and if he might need help.

A look at the calendar on his desk revealed nothing except what Will had already noted—that Rick had more free days, at least according to this, than he and Matt combined. Something about that still made him uncomfortable.

But this wasn't helping him figure out where Rick could be. Will shuffled a stack of papers around, not sure what he was looking for but feeling suspicion bubble up inside him to a degree he could no longer ignore. Something was going on at Truman Hunting Expeditions.

When he moved the next stack of paper, something fell out and clanged to the floor. He picked up a live round of ammunition much too big for caribou hunting, which was what all of their scheduled hunts had been lately. Something this big could only be used for bears.

He returned the round to the desk, careful to put it back under the stack of papers. As he did so, his hand bumped something else. It was the cartridge from the same kind of bullet—this one had been fired already and the case kept.

Had Rick, so meticulous about keeping things in order, really left these on his desk since the last time they'd taken people out after grizzlies?

Suddenly the empty calendar, the empty rifle cartridge made sense in Will's mind. Too much sense.

Rick was the one illegally hunting polar bears.

He dropped the rounds into his pocket, knowing he probably shouldn't mess with evidence but afraid to leave them unsecured. He was almost to the door when he decided he'd better leave them as proof, but snapped a picture on his phone to document that they'd been there.

Will turned back toward the door and hustled out of the building. If Rick was the one hunting the polar bears that McKenna had been investigating, and Rick hadn't made this meeting... The chances that these threads were tangling together in a way more dangerous than he'd imagined was high. Too high.

Things with McKenna and whoever was after her seemed to have escalated with the burning of the trooper post. The thought that whoever had caused the blaze—the police had ruled it arson—had meant for McKenna to be in it... He didn't want to think about that. He just thanked God that she hadn't been there.

As he climbed into his truck, Will noted a symbol on his phone saying he had a new voice mail. He hadn't noticed any missed calls. Service up here was terrible sometimes, causing him to miss calls without notification. Most of the time it was mildly frustrating at worst.

Today it made a sick feeling churn in the pit of his stomach because every time his phone rang he wondered if it was McKenna and if she needed him. He pressed the voice mail button and waited for it to connect.

His thoughts wandered, drifting to the realization that he had been thanking God for a lot more things, it seemed, since McKenna had come back into his life. Will wasn't sure if life was just better with her in it and there was more to praise God for, or if she just reminded him that life could be so much more colorful and full of joy than he made it sometimes.

"What do you want to do?" McKenna's questions from the other day, the sweet concern in her voice as she'd asked them, echoed in his mind. He didn't think he'd realized until that moment how little time he'd taken for joy since Rachael had died. He'd accused McKenna of only focusing on work, but he'd done the same thing to an even worse degree and for worse reasons.

Will swallowed hard as he checked his voice mail. The message had been sent fifteen minutes ago. From McKenna.

As he listened to McKenna's voice go from calm and informative to desperate and urgent, dread filled the pit of his stomach. He knew as she described the scene, before she seemed to realize it herself, that the car that hit her was no accident.

Whoever was after her had finally managed to get her. It may only have been fifteen minutes ago, but Will could already be fifteen minutes too late.

He gripped the steering wheel, the desire to investigate, to *find her,* overwhelming all other instincts. Will took a deep breath to steady himself, knowing this wasn't the time to rely on only his skills. He knew this wilderness, knew Rick, but Captain Wilkins knew criminals, had the training to figure out where McKenna was. Especially if Will did as McKenna had asked and got her notes. He eased his grip. He'd call the North Slope Bureau Police department and Captain Wilkins, drive to her house to get those papers, find her and help her get this case solved, the way she'd wanted. Maybe see if Matt wanted to help, too.

He could only hope McKenna's desire to solve the case didn't outweigh her desire to get out of it alive.

The first thing McKenna's mind registered was that her head was throbbing. The second was that she felt sick to her stomach. The third was that she was tied to a chair in a shack, her gun missing from the holster at her side.

Fourth and last, she realized that she was probably going to die today.

Her stomach churned. She'd been so close to making arrests and wrapping this entire thing up. She'd just needed to talk to a couple more people to confirm her suspicions. But sitting here in this little shack, which looked a lot like a hunting cabin, she was relatively certain her instincts had been right. Not that that did her any good now.

"Hello there. You're awake." Rick Truman's too-slick smile greeted her as he stepped out from the shadows in the corner where he'd been standing.

Make that 100 percent certain her instincts had been right.

"Got bored killing innocent polar bears—illegally, I might add—and decide to move on to people?" she asked with disgust.

"Are you always so quick to jump to conclusions?" He shook his head. "What about innocent until proven guilty?"

The hair on the back of her neck prickled and something in the way his eyes gleamed made her shiver. "What do you mean?"

"Who's to say I killed all those people?"

"Evidence seems to point that way." It more than *seemed* to in McKenna's opinion. She thought of the notes she'd left at her house. If she died out here, wherever she was, would Will be able to interpret her notes and pass them on to someone who could make sure justice was served?

"Circumstantial evidence." He laughed. "And it just so happens that I didn't kill them all."

McKenna said nothing.

"Not going to ask? I was sure you had more curiosity than that." More laughter. "Never mind, I'm going to tell you anyway. I'm assuming you know better than to think you're getting out of here alive."

She did know better.

"Yes, your eyes say that you understand. Good. See, those bodies you found on the tundra that first day? I didn't kill them."

"Excuse me?"

"Okay, that's not entirely true. I killed one of them. The first died in a hunting accident. It was perfectly innocent. One of his hunting buddies… He'd had a little too much to drink on the way. He got sloppy and pointed a gun in the other man's direction. It went off. He died instantly." Something like regret flickered across his face. "The shooter was torn up inside. I said there were ways we could cover it up, that no one had to know it had been his fault. He insisted he had to come clean." Regret was replaced by disdain. "He wouldn't listen. Said he had to do 'the right thing.'"

"So why did you care?" McKenna's stomach rolled at the way he talked about these men, who were dead, partially if not entirely because of Rick.

He shrugged. "I'd already started taking people on polar bear hunts by then. I couldn't afford to have the troopers snooping around because of a stupid accident and discovering that somehow. I needed that money! Besides, it's a tough business, guided hunting. The economy has hit everyone hard. Truman Hunting Expeditions has been around for a while. We're a reputable company. But all it takes is one hunting accident and tourists won't touch your company with a ten-foot pole."

McKenna could have said several things here, but she knew the man was far beyond taking responsibility for his actions. No wonder Will had seemed dissatisfied with his job and uncomfortable with how some things were handled.

"So I killed him." She saw Rick swallow hard at the memory and wondered if there was still some level of humanness in him that she could use to her advantage later. "I shot him with the other man's rifle and decided I'd get rid of the page from the log that showed they'd ever been on a trip with me. I put it away and figured if anyone ever came looking who knew for sure that they'd signed up with me, I could claim they never showed. With any luck, they'd never be found—and if they were, it would look like they'd gone out on their own and injured each other out of carelessness or anger. Something. Anything." His voice rose in volume. McKenna noted that he hadn't acted with too much of a clear plan when he'd gone to cover up his first murder. Would he be sloppy in his attempt to get rid of her? If so, it might give her a chance to get away. Or it could mean he was desperate.

"Why didn't you just walk away from the business if you're so sure it's doomed? Move away? Start a new life?"

He stared at her. "There's nowhere in the world where you could make the kind of money I stood to make with the clients I'd started to take on."

"You mean, wealthy clients who were too irresponsible to follow basic hunting-safety rules? Who wanted trophies that are illegal to obtain?"

"You wouldn't believe how much they paid if I told you.

All I wanted was to earn a little more. Then I was going to do just what you said and leave. Enjoy my money in some warm tropical paradise. And my plan was going to work. But then you showed up and started to get nosy."

Chills crawled up her arms. "I just answered a poaching call. Did you call it in?"

"What kind of idiot do you think I am? No, I didn't call it in. They were supposed to rot in the tundra, never to be heard from again."

"But *someone* called it in and then I found them."

"An unfortunate turn of events for both of us."

McKenna frowned. "But I had hardly anything to go on at that point in my investigation. I might never have pieced it all together if you hadn't kept committing crimes. So why come after me?"

"Your boyfriend had already started to poke around my business. He asked questions about the clients I was taking on. I knew it was only a matter of time before he figured something out. I thought about killing him and getting him out of my way, but he's too well known in this town. I knew I'd never get away with it. I figured it'd be easier to go after the person responsible for investigating. And when I realized you and Will knew each other..." A sinister grin inched across his face. "I thought if I attacked you, he'd be so distracted taking care of his damsel in distress that he'd leave my company alone."

"But you didn't count on Anna stumbling on to the polar bear population changes."

His face hardened. "No. I didn't count on that."

"What about Seth?"

"Who?" Rick stared blankly.

"The guy who was murdered on the beach."

Rick nodded. "Ah, him. Yes. He was a friend of the first two, apparently. He came up to investigate their deaths. He pretended he was interested in a hunting tour of his own to feel me out. Once I figured out his game, I made sure he couldn't talk, either." Desperation strained his features. "Don't you understand? I had no choice. He would have ruined everything."

McKenna finally understood. It wasn't that Rick was a cold-blooded killer. He was a greedy, selfish man who'd been forced by circumstances to make a choice. And he'd made the wrong one.

And he'd had to keep making wrong choices to cover up the wrongs he'd already done.

One more murder at this point wasn't going to make a difference to him. His conscience was already seared. He was beyond the point of no return. And he knew it.

She was going to die today.

SIXTEEN

"She's not dying today." Will slammed a fist against the inside of the passenger door of Matt's truck. Matt had insisted he was in no shape to drive.

"McKenna needs you to be calm, man. And so does my truck."

"I can't believe Truman was behind it this whole time." He hit the door again. "And we never knew."

"He hid things well. It's not your fault. McKenna went through his records and even she didn't spot anything."

"If I'd looked around more, asked more questions…"

"Then you'd be dead and not here to help."

He'd had no idea that morning that everything would come to a head today. Things had been escalating and he was ready for this nightmare to be over, for both him and McKenna, but not this way. He was afraid now to see how it would end. "We should be at the airstrip in a matter of minutes." Matt said the words as if they were supposed to reassure him. But when minutes counted like this, he couldn't help wondering if they were going fast enough.

Luke would never forgive him if he let something happen to his baby sister.

And Will would never forgive himself if he let something happen to the woman he loved…before he told her and got that knowledge into her stubborn head.

"Captain Wilkins is meeting us there, right?"

Will nodded, glancing without meaning to at the manila folder in his lap. He'd found it in the cereal box, just as McKenna had said. He marveled at the intuition, or more likely the prompting, of the Holy Spirit, that had made her leave the notes at home. This was probably what Rick had hoped to destroy in the fires, and Will knew that if Rick had gotten his hands on the notes today when he snatched McKenna, he would have destroyed the last shreds of evidence they had against him, which included some of McKenna's observations, transcripts of interviews she'd had with people and a printed version of the message Anna had sent regarding the dwindling polar bear population. A killer would be brought to justice today. Will just hoped he didn't kill again before they could catch him.

"Yeah, he's meeting us," he finally answered Matt.

"She's going to be fine," Matt said again, but the words rang just as hollow as before. The problem was that Will knew Rick's personality. He was a carefully controlled, well-thought-out man. The fact that he'd gotten this careless, this sloppy, didn't bode well for McKenna's safety.

They finally turned onto the airport's road. Will flinched when he saw the plane where his should be. It was just another reminder of the lengths to which Rick had been willing to go.

"There he is." Will pointed to a plane that met Wilkins's description. Matt parked the truck and they both hurried out, slamming the doors behind them.

"Which one is Will Harrison?" A tall man stepped out from behind the plane.

"Me."

He stuck out a hand. "Captain Bob Wilkins. Let's go. Tell me what you know on the way."

They climbed into the plane. Will wished he were flying it, but wasn't that one of the things he'd been encouraging McKenna to do—be okay with not being in control all the time?

He'd probably handled that badly, even if it was true. Apologizing for that was another thing he wished he'd have the opportunity to say to her. Would he ever have the chance to say all the things he wanted to say?

No. He wasn't giving up yet. This wasn't over.

"McKenna's been abducted by a man named Rick Truman. My former boss at—"

"Yes, Truman Hunting Expeditions." He nodded. "I've heard of it. It's a reputable company up here."

"Until recently."

The other man raised his eyebrows. "I'm going to want to hear more about that later. For now, let's focus on our search. So she's been abducted by Truman. He's an outdoorsman, so more than likely she's being held somewhere remote."

"Which doesn't narrow our search range," Will couldn't help adding.

"Obviously." Wilkins studied him. "Do you know anything else about him that could help us?"

"No." Will shook his head. "He's a hunter and he's always seemed like a decent man. I wouldn't have thought he was capable of half the things he's done."

"North Slope Bureau Police have already searched his house?"

Will nodded. "I called them as soon as I got McKenna's message and realized what had happened to her. Then I called you."

"No sign of her there?"

"No. He does have an old cabin, not too far from where the polar bear poaching was taking place."

Wilkins leaned forward. "Do you have coordinates?"

Will shook his head. "No. I've only been there once. I just remember we flew east from Barrow."

"We'll search the area." He gave instructions to the pilot and leaned back. "Truman is going to be desperate at this point."

"I know."

"You're sure you want to be involved in the search? What we find…" His voice trailed off and he shook his head, regret in his eyes. "It might not be something you'll want to see."

"She's going to be okay."

The trooper said nothing. Will fought the doubt that threatened inside of him, beyond the confident words he'd hoped were true to the deep part of himself that wasn't sure.

She *was* going to be okay. Wasn't she?

They continued flying over the tundra, the landscape empty of all but plant life and an occasional herd of caribou. They wandered freely over the land, exploring it and reminding Will of his time with McKenna, riding around on the four-wheelers.

He sat up straighter. "How would Rick have gotten her to his cabin?"

"You're on to something there." Captain Wilkins considered it. "He has a pilot's license and plane, doesn't he?"

Matt chimed in. "A plane is harder to slip away in undetected. A four-wheeler would be more likely. People leave town on those so often, no one would notice another one."

Will turned to look at his friend, who'd been silent up until then. "Thanks. I think you have a point."

He shrugged. "I told you my, uh, unique perspective might come in handy."

"Look for anything that might be an ATV trail," Captain Wilkins instructed the pilot.

Not even a minute had passed when they picked up a four-wheeler trail that brought an old hunting shack into view.

"That's it." Will's voice turned sober as he looked out at the building. If they were right, he was minutes away from seeing McKenna again. He refused to think about either the possibility of them being wrong or too late.

"There's one more thing I'd like to know." McKenna didn't know how willing Rick would be to answer more questions, but she had to at least try to stall. Then again, with all he'd confessed already, he'd made it clear that his plan was to kill her, so would answering another question matter to him?

"What's that?"

"Why didn't you kill us when you 'found—'" she used air quotes "—us after the plane crash?"

"I would have. But I'd already decided against shooting you. With the plane crash right there, there was no way to make it look like an accident." A expression of disgust crossed his features. "Besides, I've discovered that shooting people is an unpleasant experience. Animals die so much cleaner with so much less agony."

She wanted to be sick as she listened to him talk, more convinced than ever that something in this man had snapped. Neither she nor Will had thought he was the criminal type, and she'd believed they'd been right. But somewhere along the line he'd cracked and he was too far gone to reason with now. Still, the knowledge that he didn't plan to shoot her gave her a small measure of hope.

"Oh? So why not kill us on the plane somehow?"

"That phone call. I knew Will could be telling someone who you were with." He rubbed a hand up and down the back of his head, his nerves starting to show. "I can't risk anything pointing to me. It would ruin everything."

"Why not stop now?" She used the calmest voice she had to try to reason with him.

"With all I've done?" He laughed. "Getting away with this is my only hope. If I'm caught, it's all ruined. All of it. With what I've been through, I can't have that. That's why you're going to die today."

"You just said you don't like shooting people."

His menacing grin flickered. "I don't. But sometimes you do what you have to." Rick reached for his weapon. Leveled it at her. Took a breath. Then lowered it and walked out the front door of the cabin.

Minutes passed. Had he decided to leave her to die? If he was hoping animals would come after her, she stood a chance, since there was nothing to draw them. Was someone else coming to finish her off?

Whatever his plan, this was the end.

Unless she could figure a way out.

She'd been studying the layout of the cabin since they'd arrived. There wasn't much to it. One wall held the door. The next had a window. The other two were solid and she was in the corner between them. Under the window was a pallet with a sleeping bag. Beside her, a couple of feet away, was a little stove.

The first thing she needed to do was get her hands untied. If it was rope that bound her, she'd wiggle out of it somehow, but he'd used zip ties, or something like them. And she had no idea how to free herself from the hard plastic that bit against her skin.

She sat for a minute, trying to think of anything but what the next few hours would hold.

Inspiration struck as she stared into the distance wondering what to do. McKenna leaned the chair from side to side, hoping to get close enough to the stove to reach some sort of tool in the container beside it.

The chair didn't budge. She twisted her head around to look over her right shoulder and shuddered when she saw the nails attaching the chair to the wall.

He'd thought of everything.

She was truly trapped here. McKenna knew time had passed since she'd been abducted, but she didn't know how much. Hours? Days? Had Will gotten her voice mail? Would he be on his way with the notes? Or was she on her own…as she'd thought she wanted?

She'd been wrong to tell him she could do it alone. He'd tried to help, and she'd thrown it in his face.

"But it was *my* investigation. I was in charge of it," she whispered, still feeling as if she had to explain to someone, anyone, why she was on this desperate quest for independence.

Even as she said it, she knew it wasn't true.

She'd never been in charge. God had. She'd simply been the human agent carrying out His desire for justice and good to triumph. He'd brought Will to help her. He'd helped her find the leads she had uncovered. And she'd essentially told Him, just as she'd told Will, that she was fine on her own. But she wasn't. And that was okay.

As the truth overwhelmed her, she felt her shoulders sink with relief.

Now, tied to a chair, physically in control of nothing, she finally understood. McKenna knew she'd live life differently, trust God differently, with the overwhelming knowledge that He was Sovereign.

"I'm ready." Rick stepped back through the door, face grim, eyes determined, weapon ready.

It was too bad she would never get the chance.

* * *

They'd landed the plane half a mile away, hoping that putting even a small amount of distance between themselves and the cabin would camouflage their arrival.

Captain Wilkins led, motioning for Matt and Will to follow. They crept silently over the soft grasses toward the cabin.

Will could hear someone moving around inside and guessed it must be Rick. It took all the self-restraint he had not to sneak a peek through the window just overhead. But doing so could alert Rick to his presence. He couldn't afford for that to happen.

Will was weighing his options, trying to formulate a plan, when he heard voices inside the cabin.

"I'm ready."

"For what?" It was McKenna's voice. She was still alive. Her voice wavered a little and Will got the impression she cared less about getting an answer to her specific question than she did about keeping Rick talking.

"We'll go in together," Captain Wilkins whispered, motioning to the gun Will had forgotten was holstered on his hip. "Only use it if you have to. It's easier to explain me shooting if it's necessary."

Will nodded and crept closer to the door when the captain gave him the okay.

"To shoot you," Rick replied. "As I told you, I don't enjoy it, but it's the quickest and best way to make sure you don't cause me any more trouble."

As he heard the sound of the hammer being lowered on a gun, Will couldn't wait any longer. He threw open the door of the cabin, noticing that neither Wilkins nor Matt had followed. Rick's gun had been leveled at McKenna, who had her eyes squeezed shut, but he whirled at the noise and the gun went with him, pointing instead straight at Will.

"You." Rick's eyes narrowed. "You are ruining everything. You and your nosy girlfriend."

"You made your own choices. We didn't do this to you," Will said as he stepped closer, working to put himself between McKenna and Rick's weapon. He tried to catch McKenna's eye, to reassure her that he was doing everything he could to make sure they got out of this somehow, but she was looking at something behind him. Wilkins and Matt?

"But I had a plan," Rick whined.

Will noticed Rick's voice seemed different—more desperate than usual. Every muscle in Will's body tensed, waiting for whatever would happen next.

"And it will still work fine," Rick said as though he'd just realized, a smile crossing his face. "I can just shoot you, too. Yes, that works nicely." He turned back to McKenna. "But I'll shoot her first."

He started to raise the gun again.

Will reached for his weapon, keeping Captain Wilkins's instructions in mind but knowing if it came down to it, he'd do what he had to do to keep McKenna alive.

"Put the gun down."

Wilkins's calm voice coming from behind him was not what Will expected to hear. He glanced back to see that the man had pulled his own gun and was pointing it at Rick. Personally he would have shot first and tried to reason with the guy later, but Wilkins was the pro. Nonetheless, Will kept his hand near his holster, heart racing as he waited to see how this was going to go down.

He didn't have to wait long. The moment Rick caught sight of a trooper uniform, he shot the man in the chest.

The sharp crack exploded in one quick burst and then there was silence again.

Captain Wilkins crumpled to the floor, blood pooling under him. Will fought waves of nausea that mixed with adrenaline and threatened to overwhelm him. Matt, who'd stayed outside until then, came around the doorway, looking ready to help in any way he could.

"Anyone else want to threaten me?" Rick asked, waving his gun around wildly. His self-control was deteriorating by the second and the situation along with it. Will looked down at the trooper on the ground, unsure if he was dead or just would be soon.

"You're a coward," McKenna said, cold steel in her voice.

Will tensed, knowing this was his chance. He caught Matt's eye and nodded. As Rick turned to look at McKenna, Will jumped him from behind, attempting with Matt's help to wrestle him to the ground and disarm him. Somewhere in the scuffle, Matt got punched and let go. Will held tight and had almost succeeded in getting Rick's gun when Rick landed a punch hard against his jaw, jerking away from Will's hold as he fought to pull himself out of a daze.

"That was just stupid," he said with disdain, wiping blood off his own face. "That's it. This whole thing has lasted long enough and I'm done."

Rick's eyes were wild as he looked over the group of them, apparently deciding who he was going to shoot next.

"You got close to ruining my life, McKenna Clark. Now, unfortunately, you have to pay with yours." Before Will had a chance to react, Rick had his gun out and aimed, straight at McKenna.

This time he pulled the trigger.

The noise of the shot sounded almost as if it had an

echo. Will realized why as he watched Rick fall to the ground. He'd been shot, too, from somewhere outside the cabin. Likely with a rifle, judging by the impact. He lay still on the floor. Will watched his unmoving chest. He was dead.

Threat assessed, he looked back up at McKenna, who was still tied to the chair. Her eyes were wide and fixed on the bullet hole in the wall of the cabin less than an inch from where her head had been.

"He missed." Her voice was a mix of panic and awe. Relief and sheer terror.

He knew exactly how she felt. "I can't tell you how happy that makes me." He longed to untie her, pull her into his arms and never, ever let her go.

But someone was outside the cabin with a high-powered rifle. Whoever it was had shot Rick, so hopefully that made that person an ally, but Will needed to know for sure. He looked through the window but didn't see anything.

Will wasn't taking any chances with McKenna's life. "I'm going outside to see who that was."

"Don't leave," her eyes and voice both pleaded.

"I have to." He hesitated at the door. "I know this isn't the best time to say this. But just in case…"

"In case nothing." She was firm. "You're coming back."

He met her eyes. "I love you, McKenna."

Then he stepped outside, closed the door behind him and pulled his pistol from its holster, holding it in a ready position.

"Don't shoot," a familiar voice called.

He turned in the direction it had come from, catching sight of someone dressed in camo.

"Chris." Will lowered the gun slightly but kept it out. "You shot Rick?"

"Yes. Is he dead?"

"Yes. Mind telling me why you're here?"

"I saw him abduct McKenna."

"And you didn't call the troopers? The police? Anyone?"

"I didn't know who I could trust. It's a long story."

Will studied him for a long minute, praying that God would give him wisdom. He believed Chris was on their side. "All right. Go on in. We need to untie McKenna and see if Captain Wilkins is still alive."

They opened the door and Matt looked up from where he knelt beside Wilkins, his face grim. "He's still hanging on. But he needs to get out of here now."

"Or he needs someone to come to him." Chris pulled a SAT phone from the backpack he carried and handed it to Will. "Call whoever you want, just so you know this isn't some kind of trick." He said the last words to McKenna, who Will noted was watching him with suspicion.

"What are you doing here?" she asked, eyes narrowed.

"Saving your life."

Will gave the emergency dispatcher a summary of their situation and Wilkins's condition and hung up after they promised a flight would be on its way to their GPS location as soon as possible. "He says he can explain," Will told McKenna as he handed the phone back to Chris.

"Go ahead," McKenna replied. "This, I've got to hear."

SEVENTEEN

"Several of the native Alaskans had come to me," Chris began, shifting his weight from one foot to the other. "I guess they felt the last trooper wasn't taking their concerns seriously. They know how to keep tabs on animal populations and they weren't satisfied with the job the last guy did. I flew the trooper everywhere, tried to watch him closely, but I never could decide if he was corrupt or just incompetent. When they sent you, an inexperienced city girl, up here, I thought for sure someone had someone in the troopers in their pocket. I figured that sending you up here was their way to ensure that regulations weren't strictly enforced and things continued to slip through the cracks."

"So you *were* following me." She'd been sure of it ever since she'd talked to him at the pizza place, but it was nice to hear him say the words.

"I was. But that's all I did."

"I know."

Will broke in. "And it's good he was following you because he saw Rick cause the crash and abduct you."

The debt she owed Chris was greater than she'd realized. "I misjudged you," she confessed. The words, the admission that she'd been so zealous to do her job right that she'd isolated someone who could have been a huge help in the case, pained her. But it was true.

"Same here. If you ever need anything else, let me know."

"Will's going to be busy soon starting up his own company. Any chance you know where I could find a good pilot?"

He grinned as he stuck out his hand. "Give me a call anytime."

McKenna took his hand and shook it, her grip firm. "I'll do that."

"You two probably want to talk alone," Chris said, eyeing her and Will.

"We'll stay with Wilkins," Matt offered. He nodded toward the exit. McKenna got the message and turned to Will.

"Want to take a walk with me?"

He nodded, and followed her out the door.

McKenna's pulse sped up to racing speed. The case had been an almost physical barrier against getting involved with Will beyond friendship. She'd been able to limit her thoughts about him, reminding herself that being distracted could cost her life. But that wasn't an issue now. And she knew she wasn't crazy to think that he might feel something for her, too. His words earlier, along with that kiss on the tundra, had proven it. They'd just never had the chance to finish that conversation.

The thought of having it scared her. But so did the thought of not having it. It was time to resolve this, too. She was running out of excuses.

"I am so glad you're okay," Will said again. He'd thought so many things when she'd gone missing. Several of those thoughts were possibilities of what could have happened to her—things he never wanted to think about again. Right now she was standing in front of him looking healthy, unharmed and entirely too kissable. And while the moment seemed entirely inappropriate for things like kissing, he wasn't sure he was going to be able to stop himself.

"About yesterday…" he continued. "I got your message. It's okay, McKenna." He wrapped one arm around her, then the other, slowly pulling her closer to him.

She swiped a tear from her eye. "But it's not okay. I can't believe I pushed you away like that."

"I was too protective." Will shrugged, knowing now how true the words were. "I should have let you handle the case."

McKenna sniffed.

"But whatever it is you've been trying to prove, McKenna, you can stop. You've proven it." He tightened his grip on her, not caring that activity swarmed around them, that planes had started to land near them with paramedics to treat Wilkins and various law enforcement officers ready to process the scene, or that they were standing yards away from a crime scene. "You're a grown woman and an incredible trooper and I have been guilty of underestimating you. You *don't* need me. But I love you. Even if you are Luke's little sister. And I'm hoping you love me enough to let me take care of you for the rest of our lives even if you could do just fine on your own."

She sniffed. "No."

Will's heart dropped a thousand feet in that split second and he struggled to swallow past the lump in his throat. "No?"

"I mean, not 'no' to the whole thing. 'No,' you're wrong. I do need you. I needed you today and I've always needed you, Will." She sniffed again. "I was wrong to push you away—the same way I pushed God away—and I was wrong to think I could handle everything on my own."

Will tightened his arms around her, loving the feeling of her relaxing into him.

"What are you doing with your arms around my sister, Harrison?"

Will laughed at the familiar voice and the fact that McKenna pulled away when she heard it. "I think the better question is, what are you doing interrupting?"

"Luke!" McKenna pulled away from Will and threw her arms around her brother, who had stepped out of one of the small planes that had just landed. "What are you doing here? Isn't this a little ways out of your jurisdiction?"

"I got a call from a trooper friend of mine who heard about what happened this morning. I came straight out to find you, but I wasn't in Barrow for long before word came that you were out here. So I talked them into letting me on the plane." He shook his head. "Abducted, McKenna?"

She shrugged.

Luke laughed as he hugged her again. "I'm so glad you're okay, kid. But wow, am I proud of you."

"Thanks."

The three of them stood for a minute, staring wordlessly at the chaos that had erupted around them.

"I know everything," McKenna finally said. "Rick confessed to it all."

"To everything?" Will asked.

She nodded.

"By the way, I checked in with the crime lab this morning," Luke told her. "They were just finishing getting your results together." He nodded toward the cabin. "They found DNA that doesn't belong to the victims. I'm willing to bet once they get Rick to Anchorage and take a sample, it'll be a perfect match."

McKenna nodded. "I'll just be glad to have all this behind us."

A paramedic ran toward them then, and Will braced himself for one more bit of bad news, but as the guy got closer, he started to smile. "The captain is going to be okay. You got us here in time."

"Thank you!" McKenna called. The man waved and ran back to the helicopter that would take Captain Wilkins to Anchorage and better medical care.

"Looks like everything's turning out well, after all." Luke nodded. A slow smile inched across his face. "For everyone."

Will nodded at his friend, knowing that nod and smile said he approved of Will pursuing a relationship with McKenna, or at least didn't disapprove. He should have asked sooner. But he knew that God had perfect timing. And this seemed to be the timing for his and McKenna's relationship to grow. He glanced over at her but didn't see the same peace on her face that he was feeling.

"What is it?" he asked, wondering if he'd had anything to do with her frown.

"Nothing." She shook her head. "Just the case."

"Let's get out of here," Luke said. "You don't need to be reliving it all. There's no reason you can't talk to the team working this once you're back in Barrow. Especially since it was your case to start with. Come on, my buddy will fly us." He motioned toward one of the planes at the edge of the cluster.

"I think that's a good idea." Will grabbed McKenna's hand and led her to the plane.

They'd been sitting in Will's living room for an hour when McKenna finally found the words for what had been bothering her. "I sat there in that cabin and listened to his whole confession. But what I still don't understand is why. Why would Rick do that? Why would anyone go to such violent lengths?" McKenna asked, processing her questions as she vocalized them.

"Money," Luke and Will answered instantly.

"But it's just money." She frowned. "I can see a decent man breaking the law for it, but not going all the way to murder."

Luke shrugged. "It's almost textbook. People always have the capacity for evil, if they choose to take that route."

"Which is why we need a Savior," Will added.

A look McKenna didn't understand passed over Luke's face. She'd have to ask him about that later. But she knew Will was right.

Rick had made his choices. She had to get the look on his face out of her mind and let it go. McKenna took a deep breath and prayed that God would help her, thankful that in not too many hours, her life and job would both settle down.

"I'll be so glad when my job gets back to normal," she said with a sigh.

Luke cleared his throat. "So, are you staying in Barrow?" He directed the question to her.

McKenna's heart began to race and she felt herself tense in preparation for the coming conversation.

"What do you mean?" Will asked slowly.

"You didn't tell him?"

McKenna shook her head slightly. Luke stood. "I'll be outside." He patted his leg for Mollie to follow, and after a long glance at her owner, she did so. The door shut behind them, leaving the house utterly silent until McKenna spoke again.

"Nothing's official yet. But it's possible I could get a job back in Anchorage. It's the same level as what I have

now, so I'd keep my last promotion, but it's in the city."
Her old boss in Anchorage had called her not long after
they'd arrived back in Barrow. He'd said it would take a
few days to process and make it official, but that he'd had
an unexpected opening just days ago and given how she'd
handled herself for this case, she was his first choice to
fill the vacancy.

"So…you're leaving."

He said it as a statement not a question. There was no
emotion in his tone, no indication that he wanted her to
stay. Just a statement of fact, as if he should have known
that was what she would do.

"Did I say that?"

"I thought—"

"You didn't think. Not if you automatically assumed I'd
be leaving." McKenna felt her cheeks heating, a telltale
sign that her temper was flaring. She took a deep breath
to calm herself down.

"Isn't that what you want?"

She said nothing. The job in Anchorage *was* what she
wanted, if she didn't factor Will into the equation. But
she *wanted* to factor him in—for the rest of her life. She
thought everything that had happened after the rescue
meant they were a couple. But if he thought she was leaving without talking to him first, maybe she'd misunder-
stood.

"If you had a say…what would you say about me trans-
ferring?" she finally asked.

"You really have to ask that?" Will said as he moved to
where she sat on the sofa and grabbed her hand.

She blinked away the tears that threatened. "Maybe."

He tightened his grip on her hand. "Then if I had a say,
I'd say that I love you. I'd say that I want you to stay here

with me, out here in this crazy wilderness, having all kinds of adventures until we're too old to remember them."

McKenna's smile grew, spreading from inside her heart, all the way across her face. "So you don't mind if I stay?"

"It would make me the happiest man in the world."

"About that kiss you weren't sure if you should apologize for..." She trailed off.

"Yes?" he whispered, inching closer.

"You do need to apologize...for taking so long." McKenna tilted her face up until her lips met his and they shared the kind of kiss that only comes from a deep love born out of friendship.

"Now, what about my question?" He pulled back, searching her eyes for their answer. They sparkled beneath raised eyebrows.

"A question?" A slow smile inched across McKenna's face. "I don't think I heard you ask a question."

He smiled back. "Do I really have to ask?"

She nodded. "I've been dreaming of this for decades. I'm not letting you get away with not being official."

"Let me try this again, then." He took her hands in his and knelt down on one knee. "McKenna Clark, you've been driving me crazy and making me fall in love with you I think since you could talk. And I want to love you and take care of you and keep getting to know you forever. Will you marry me?"

"I can't think of anything that sounds better."

"Ready to go?"

McKenna looked down at the sparkling diamond-and-gold wedding band adorning her left hand. It had only taken a month to pull together details for a wedding and get their families up to Barrow to watch it happen. Some people had wondered what the rush was, but McKenna and

Will were sure this was right and saw no reason to wait even longer than they already had.

She looked up at the man who had captured her heart so many years ago, who'd only grown more dear to her as time went on.

"Almost. I have to say goodbye to a few people first."

Will laughed. "We'll only be gone for a week."

Will had arranged for the two of them to fly to a remote resort and spa near Mount McKinley for their honeymoon. It was outside a little town called Talkeetna, and was enough in the wilderness to make Will happy and was upscale and luxurious enough to satisfy all McKenna's fantasies of being pampered.

"That's true. And I can't wait to leave with you." She smiled and looked out at the small group of friends and family who were still standing around talking and enjoying cake. "But it's polite to tell people goodbye. They did come here for us, you know." She grinned and then felt her smile slip. "Besides, Anna's moving away while we're gone."

"I'd forgotten that. Take as much time as you need." He stroked her arm as he stepped away from her. "But remember, this next week? You're all mine."

McKenna's face heated and she smiled at her new husband, then walked to where she saw her friend standing.

"I can't believe you're leaving Barrow," McKenna said to Anna as she hugged her.

Anna shrugged, the slow movement of her shoulder evidence of the long healing process she was still enduring since being shot. "It's time." She shook her head. "I've thought before about going, living somewhere else, having a little adventure of my own for a long time now. Since I got shot...I'm ready for a new start."

"So where will you go?" McKenna asked with genuine concern for the woman who'd so willingly opened her home to her and her heart to her friendship.

"Probably Anchorage." She laughed. "Isn't this a switch? You're happily settling into small-town life, and I'm off to the big city."

McKenna couldn't help laughing, too. "It's funny how things work out sometimes."

"It is. I'm hoping to find a good job there at one of the hospitals. Something nice and predictable. More than anything, I just want to feel safe again."

"I'll be praying you do."

Anna walked away and McKenna looked over at Will, who looked so handsome in his tux. "We can say goodbye and head out now. I don't want to make the pilot wait for us," she teased.

They bid their friends and family farewell and walked outside amidst snowflakes that fell from the sky like their own little shower of confetti.

"Will we make it to the resort tonight?" McKenna asked as she climbed into the plane, noting the storm that had moved in.

"It's not a bad storm, we should be fine." Will looked at her with a slow smile. "But there's no one I'd rather be stranded in the tundra with than you."

McKenna laughed. She couldn't have agreed more.

* * * * *

Dear Reader,

It's because of your love for reading that I have the opportunity to do what I love—write—and I am so grateful to you for that. Thank you!

I hope you enjoyed Will and McKenna's story. When I first started brainstorming a story about a wildlife trooper, I knew she'd be stubborn and determined to prove herself, and I knew she'd be falling in love with a childhood friend. I had a wonderful time writing and seeing all the other details of this story unfold as it progressed. I especially enjoyed the setting for this book—I lived in Alaska for nine years and it is one of my favorite places on earth. The entire state is a stunning combination of beauty that's difficult to describe and a little bit of danger that comes from it being the last frontier. It's an untamed land—ready for adventurers. Everyone should visit at least once.

In this story, both Will and McKenna come to grips with the sovereignty of God and realize that they aren't in control—either of their own lives or the lives of those they love. It's a truth I've wrestled with before (to say I like to be in charge is a bit of an understatement...), but it's a truth that will set you free, if you let it, and give you peace. I pray that something in this book challenged you to trust God more in your own life, as it challenged me during the writing to trust Him with mine.

I'd love to hear from you! You can get in touch with me through email, sarahvarland@gmail.com, or find me on my personal blog, espressoinalatteworld.blogspot.com. Also if you're interested in writing, or a behind-the-scenes look at a writer's brain, come visit some of my author friends and me at scribblechicks.blogspot.com.

Sarah Varland

Questions for Discussion

1. At the beginning of the story, McKenna is given the job of investigating the murders on the tundra, something that's outside her comfort zone. When have you had to step out of your comfort zone? Is this something you find easy or difficult?

2. McKenna's relationship with God in the beginning of the story is rather "hands-off." She doesn't see any need to bother Him unless she needs something really important. How do we know from the Bible that God *wants* to be involved in all areas of our lives?

3. Will points out that McKenna has issues trusting God. In what ways does McKenna struggle with trusting God? How do you see Will having this same struggle—though it takes longer for him to recognize it in himself?

4. Will and McKenna were friends before they fell in love. Do you believe the best love stories start with friends? Or do you believe in love at first sight?

5. McKenna suspects Will's friend Matt at one point because of his past. Has something in your past changed the way people look at you? Have you ever viewed someone differently because of a past mistake they made? How can we move beyond the past in our lives or in the lives of others?

6. Will realizes that he tends to *over*protect those he loves. Is this something you do? How do we find a

balance between protecting and taking care of those we love and trusting their care to God?

7. Rick was a decent guy at the beginning of the book whose greed got away with him. Why is greed so dangerous?

8. McKenna learns during the story that it's okay for her to rely on others for help and not insist on being independent all the time. Do you lean more toward being someone who likes to handle everything alone without help? Or do you prefer to have others on your team?

9. Will struggles to release the past and acknowledge that Rachael's death was not his fault. Has there been a time that you felt responsible for something that wasn't in your control? How can you keep from feeling this way?

10. When Rick confesses his crimes to McKenna, he explains that everything started when he wanted to try to cover up his illegal polar bear hunting trips. Have you ever attempted to hide something (good or bad) and then kept having to go further in your attempts to cover it up? What did you learn from the experience?

11. Were you surprised that Chris was the one to save McKenna in the end, given the way he'd treated her? Have you ever received help from an unlikely source in your life?

12. Which character did you identify most with in this story? How are you alike? Which was the hardest for you to relate to?

COMING NEXT MONTH FROM
Love Inspired® Suspense

Available November 4, 2014

DEADLY HOLIDAY REUNION
by Lenora Worth

Jake Cavanaugh's daughter has been kidnapped by a serial killer, and the only person he can turn to for help is Ella Terrell, a former FBI agent...and his old high school sweetheart.

HAZARDOUS HOMECOMING
Wings of Danger • by Dana Mentink

A found necklace reopens an old missing persons case and changes everything for Ruby Hudson and Cooper Stokes. They must put the past behind them in order to find the truth before someone silences them.

TWIN THREAT CHRISTMAS
by Rachelle McCalla

Long-lost twin sisters have a chance to reunite at Christmastime if they can stay alive long enough to find each other.

SILENT NIGHT STANDOFF
First Responders • by Susan Sleeman

The last person Skyler Brennan wants to spend Christmas Eve with is her FBI agent ex-boyfriend, but she'll have to trust him with her life—and heart—when a bank robber comes after her seeking revenge.

IDENTITY WITHHELD
by Sandra Orchard

A widowed firefighter is determined to rescue a woman in witness protection from her pursuers. But when the criminals involve his son, will he be able to save them both?

PERILOUS REFUGE
by Kathleen Tailer

After witnessing a murder, Chelsea Rogers goes on the run. Can she trust Alex Sullivan to protect her from the killer on her trail—before she becomes the next victim?

———————

LISCNM1014

REQUEST YOUR FREE BOOKS!

2 FREE RIVETING INSPIRATIONAL NOVELS
PLUS 2 FREE MYSTERY GIFTS

Love Inspired®
SUSPENSE

YES! Please send me 2 FREE Love Inspired® Suspense novels and my 2 FREE mystery gifts (gifts are worth about $10). After receiving them, if I don't wish to receive any more books, I can return the shipping statement marked "cancel." If I don't cancel, I will receive 4 brand-new novels every month and be billed just $4.74 per book in the U.S. or $5.24 per book in Canada. That's a savings of at least 21% off the cover price. It's quite a bargain! Shipping and handling is just 50¢ per book in the U.S. and 75¢ per book in Canada.* I understand that accepting the 2 free books and gifts places me under no obligation to buy anything. I can always return a shipment and cancel at any time. Even if I never buy another book, the two free books and gifts are mine to keep forever.

123/323 IDN F5AC

Name _____ (PLEASE PRINT) _____

Address _____ Apt. # _____

City _____ State/Prov. _____ Zip/Postal Code _____

Signature (if under 18, a parent or guardian must sign) _____

Mail to the **Harlequin® Reader Service:**
IN U.S.A.: P.O. Box 1867, Buffalo, NY 14240-1867
IN CANADA: P.O. Box 609, Fort Erie, Ontario L2A 5X3

**Are you a current subscriber to Love Inspired Suspense books
and want to receive the larger-print edition?
Call 1-800-873-8635 or visit www.ReaderService.com.**

* Terms and prices subject to change without notice. Prices do not include applicable taxes. Sales tax applicable in N.Y. Canadian residents will be charged applicable taxes. Offer not valid in Quebec. This offer is limited to one order per household. Not valid for current subscribers to Love Inspired Suspense books. All orders subject to credit approval. Credit or debit balances in a customer's account(s) may be offset by any other outstanding balance owed by or to the customer. Please allow 4 to 6 weeks for delivery. Offer available while quantities last.

Your Privacy—The Harlequin® Reader Service is committed to protecting your privacy. Our Privacy Policy is available online at www.ReaderService.com or upon request from the Harlequin Reader Service.
We make a portion of our mailing list available to reputable third parties that offer products we believe may interest you. If you prefer that we not exchange your name with third parties, or if you wish to clarify or modify your communication preferences, please visit us at www.ReaderService.com/consumerschoice or write to us at Harlequin Reader Service Preference Service, P.O. Box 9062, Buffalo, NY 14269. Include your complete name and address.

LIS13R

Love Inspired
SUSPENSE
RIVETING INSPIRATIONAL ROMANCE

HAZARDOUS HOMECOMING

by

DANA MENTINK

Cooper Stokes returns to Oregon just as an explosive case rocks the town. New evidence surfaces in the twenty-year-old disappearance of a neighborhood child, but the same suspect remains—his brother. As Cooper wants to prove his brother's innocence, Ruby Hudson wants justice for her missing friend—and an end to the nightmare that haunts her. But seeing Cooper again is a dream come true. Long ago they shared an attraction, till family shame drove him away. Amid danger and deception, can this be their second chance? But the deeper they dig into decades-old secrets, the closer they get to an abductor who'll do anything to remain in the shadows....

***Available November 2014 wherever
Love Inspired books and ebooks are sold.***